She peeled off the crimson wrapping and opened a small box. It contained a round silver Christmas ornament.

Rue held it up so Cody could see. "What am I going to do with this? I don't have a tree. I can't even go to my house because it's too dangerous for me to be alone."

"You have a home with me," he said.

His smile was gentle and warm. When he reached over and stroked her cheek, some of the ache went away. Right now, he was her haven. "My protector."

He winked. "Somebody's got to watch over you."

And she was grateful. If he hadn't been here, she'd be lonely *and* in danger.

"Have you been able to talk with anyone about the case?"

"Tomorrow. It's going to have to wait until tomorrow."

"What are we going to do for the rest of today?"

"I have plans." His grin widened and he winked. "Get ready."

"For what?"

"Tonight, we'r̶ ̶ ̶ ̶ ̶ ̶ ̶ ̶ ̶ ̶ ̶ ̶ ̶ ̶ ̶ ̶ ̶ merry little Christm̶

CASSIE MILES

CHRISTMAS COVER-UP

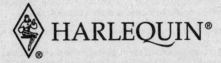

TORONTO • NEW YORK • LONDON
AMSTERDAM • PARIS • SYDNEY • HAMBURG
STOCKHOLM • ATHENS • TOKYO • MILAN • MADRID
PRAGUE • WARSAW • BUDAPEST • AUCKLAND

To Gary Outlaw and the guys, especially Bernice.
And, as always, to Rick.

ISBN-13: 978-0-373-69292-7
ISBN-10:   0-373-69292-7

CHRISTMAS COVER-UP

www.eHarlequin.com

Printed in U.S.A.

ABOUT THE AUTHOR

For Cassie Miles, the best part about writing a story set in Eagle County near the Vail ski area is the ready-made excuse to head into the mountains for research. Though the winter snows are great for skiing, her favorite season is fall when the aspens turn gold.

The rest of the time Cassie lives in Denver where she takes urban hikes around Cheesman Park, reads a ton and critiques often. Her current plans include a Vespa and a road trip, despite eye-rolling objections from her adult children.

Books by Cassie Miles

HARLEQUIN INTRIGUE

826—ROCKY MOUNTAIN MANHUNT*
832—ROCKY MOUNTAIN MANEUVERS*
874—WARRIOR SPIRIT
904—UNDERCOVER COLORADO**
910—MURDER ON THE MOUNTAIN**
948—FOOTPRINTS IN THE SNOW
978—PROTECTIVE CONFINEMENT†
984—COMPROMISED SECURITY†
999—NAVAJO ECHOES
1025—CHRISTMAS COVER-UP

*Colorado Crime Consultants
**Rocky Mountain Safe House
†Safe House: Mesa Verde

CAST OF CHARACTERS

Rue (Ruth Ann) Harris—Struggling to make a go of her custom cake shop, the last thing she needs is to witness a high-profile murder. Or to fall in love.

Cody Berringer—The ruthless corporate attorney has a vulnerable spot when it comes to the twenty-year-old unsolved murder of his father, "Lucky Ted."

Leticia Grant-Harris-Mason-Lopez-Jones-Wyndemere—Now a wedding planner, Rue's mother never met a man she wouldn't marry.

Danny Mason—Leticia's second husband, the newly elected but not sworn-in mayor of Denver is the closest to a father Rue ever had.

Bob Lindahl—Danny's old friend and political supporter.

Mike Blanco—Another of Danny's friends, he's a former cop who suffers from serious heart ailments.

Jerome Samuels—Danny's campaign manager, who pulled himself out of the gang life to become supremely ambitious.

Tyler Zubek—A witness to the murder, he's in the wrong place at the wrong time.

Carlos—Lindahl's bodyguard is injured in the murder.

Madigan—His criminal record makes him the police's number one suspect.

Bernice Layne—Rue's colorful assistant at the cake shop has a heart of gold and a wardrobe to match.

Chapter One

Shortly after Rue Harris opened her custom bakery shop, she realized that she was going to need a lot more dough.

Though her profits from the morning pastry sales were decent, the real money came from providing designer cakes for big events. She had to publicize, to build her reputation. Which was why she had agreed to provide two free cakes for a political event on a Thursday, one week after Thanksgiving.

The purpose of this midafternoon party was to thank those who had contributed to the campaign of Danny Mason, the newly elected mayor of Denver. Danny was Rue's former stepfather. One of several. Her mother had been married five times.

Though it was early for Christmas, that was today's theme. The huge ballroom in a foothills mansion was festooned with wreaths and red velvet bows. A fifteen-foot-tall Christmas tree stood in the cathedral-style window, and the caterer's staff wore

Santa hats and holly pins. A very tall Santa Claus in full beard and suit meandered through the crowd making ho-ho-ho noises.

Rue reached up to tuck a wisp of brown hair into her high ponytail, then adjusted the shoulder strap of her burgundy chef's apron so her white embroidered logo—Ruth Ann's Cakes—would be visible. Nervously, she shuffled her weight from one foot to the other. *Come on, Rue. Mingle.* Her main reason for being here was to make contacts, and it wasn't doing her any good to be a wallflower. She needed to meet people.

Her gaze skimmed the ballroom. Danny had once been a cop, and she spotted a couple of navy blue police uniforms in the crowd. Some of these people she'd met before but most were friends of Bob Lindahl, the owner of this mansion. Lindahl was a building contractor with a shady reputation that made her wonder how many of these guests—cops or otherwise—were carrying guns.

None of my business. If she happened to pick up a few new clients who were criminals, so be it. She'd run a special on cakes with files baked inside—the perfect surprise for a jailed felon.

She launched herself into the crowd, prepared to mingle, mingle, mingle. She said a couple of hellos, introduced herself to strangers, checked out the baubles on the Christmas tree and bobbed her head in time to the music from the jazz combo playing Christmas tunes.

When she glanced back toward the serving line, the caterer seemed to be almost ready for her. The red-draped table on the far right end was saved for her cakes. Time to bring them in from the van, but first she needed to wash her hands.

She slipped through a door at the edge of the ballroom, hoping it was a bathroom.

It wasn't.

And she was not alone.

The tall Santa stood in the center of an oriental rug in a study. He was unbuttoning his red jacket.

"Sorry," she said as she reached for the door handle. "I was looking for…a quiet space."

"Me, too," he said. "Peace and quiet and cool air. I've been wearing this suit for an hour, and it's hot."

"Not like the North Pole, huh?"

He stuck out his hand. "I'm Cody Berringer." Peering over his fluffy white beard, he stared at her chest and read the embroidery. "You must be Ruth Ann's Cakes."

"That's me," she said as she shook his hand. "I'm Rue Harris, and I make custom cakes for any occasion."

"Weddings?"

"Are you getting married?"

"Not me," he said with the shudder of a confirmed bachelor. "The cake would be for my little sister."

He peeled off the Santa jacket. Underneath he wore a sleeveless T-shirt and a giant pillow stuck into fuzzy red trousers that were held up by suspenders. She noticed a suit and shirt tossed over the back of the sofa. Surely, he didn't intend to change clothes right in front of her.

He asked, "What else should I know about you, Rue Harris? Have you been naughty or nice?"

In usual circumstances, she would have made a hasty retreat before the Santa Claus striptease went any farther, but she was here to mingle and he'd already mentioned a wedding cake. Cody Berringer was a potential customer.

"Naughty or nice," she mused. "Shouldn't I be sitting on your lap when you ask that question?"

"That sounds a little bit naughty."

"You're kind of a bad Santa, aren't you?"

"I try."

When he pulled out the pillow, his costume deflated. He had muscular shoulders and long, lean arms. His height was impressive, well over six feet. He towered over her. A dominating presence.

Mesmerized, she watched as he yanked off his fur-trimmed red hat and ran his fingers through his thick black hair.

Then he removed the beard.

Rue felt her eyes widen. She pressed her lips together to keep from gaping like the village idiot. Cody Berringer was gorgeous. Square jaw. Full lips. And the sexiest blue eyes she'd ever seen.

He sat on a white leather sofa and started digging through his Santa bag. "I'm not much of a Santa. Wasn't giving anything away. I was collecting donations for Hathaway House, a homeless shelter."

"You're an idealist." Gorgeous *and* sensitive?

"Not a chance." He chuckled—not with a ho-ho-ho but a real laugh. "I'm a lawyer."

"Which doesn't necessarily mean that you're a shark. Lots of lawyers are idealistic."

"Good for them," he said as he stacked the checks and pledge cards from his Santa bag.

She really hoped he wasn't a sleaze. "Do you work for Bob Lindahl?"

"I'm not one of Bob's boys," he said with a sneer. "My expertise is corporate law—take-overs and mergers. Using your shark analogy, I think of myself as a great white. Not a bottom feeder."

"I'll take your word for it." She gave him a smile.

He didn't smile back. "You like to think the best of people, don't you?"

His cynical tone made optimism sound like a negative trait. "I'm not naive."

"Sure, you are. Sweet and sunny."

She adjusted her opinion of him, adding arrogant to the list. "For your information, I can be very bitter. Like dark chocolate."

His intensely blue eyes focused sharply. "Have we met before, Rue?"

"I don't think so." With her snub nose and muddy gray eyes, she had the kind of face that reminded people of someone else. Her only remarkable feature was her long, thick, chestnut hair which she usually kept pulled up in a ponytail. "But I've lived in Denver most of my life so we might have run into each other somewhere along the line."

"There's something familiar about you." When he stood and came toward her, her senses prickled. He was dangerously sexy, radiating masculine energy. It took all her willpower not to step back as he approached. He leaned closer, inches away from her cheek. "You smell great. Like butter and vanilla."

"A cake-baker's perfume."

"How are you connected to the campaign?" His tone was confrontational, as if she were a witness on the stand. "What's your opinion of our new mayor?"

"He's my former stepfather." Explaining her family history was always complicated. "He was my mother's second husband."

"Then, you're not such an innocent. You grew up in a family of sharks."

"Danny's a good guy," she said defensively. He filled the fatherhood role far better than the man who was named on her birth certificate. "He coached my Little League team and taught me to swim."

"Is that when he was a police officer?"

"One of Denver's finest."

"My dad knew him back then."

She sensed an undercurrent of tension—something in the way he said "my dad." This casual conversation had taken on an air of importance.

"My father's name," he said, "was Ted Berringer. He was an assistant district attorney. They called him Lucky Ted. Did you know him?"

Her mind flashed back twenty years to when she was six years old. Lucky Ted Berringer? She remembered Danny and her mother talking about him in one of those grown-up dinner-table discussions that got her banished from the room. The name—Lucky Ted—stuck in her mind because he didn't sound lucky at all. "Your father was killed."

The glow from his eyes sharpened to blue laser pinpoints, boring into her skull with such intensity that he must be reading her mind. Not that he'd find anything terribly interesting. Her life was simple, and she worked hard to keep it that way. Calm. Stable. Steady.

She suspected that Cody was the one with secrets. There was something dark and troubled about him. Something that warned her to keep her distance.

"My father's murder," he said, "was never solved."

"I'm sorry."

"You would have approved of him. He was an idealist."

Ending his scrutiny, Cody stepped away from her and went to the sofa where he picked up a white tailored shirt and shook the wrinkles from it. "I'd like to see you again, Rue."

From the pocket of her apron, she produced a business card which she placed on the coffee table beside the pile of checks and pledges. "About the cake for your sister's wedding?"

"We'll discuss the cake over dinner. Saturday night."

"A date?"

"Sure, you can call it a date."

She was shocked. Guys like him didn't date

women like her. Hotshot corporate lawyers went for more flashy partners—sexy blondes in low-cut gowns, reeking of expensive perfume.

Even if Cody actually was interested in her, why would he assume she was free? That she didn't have a current boyfriend? "After I check my schedule, I can—"

"I'll call you with the time."

He turned away from her.

Apparently, she was being dismissed. That was his last word. Could he possibly be more egotistical? She had half a mind to tell him that she wouldn't be home when he called. No matter how handsome he was. No matter how many cakes he might order.

Calmly, he slipped off one of his suspenders. The red trousers sagged. Rue didn't want to stay for the rest of the Santa striptease; she'd seen quite enough of Cody Berringer for one day. She pivoted quickly and left.

As soon as she entered the ballroom, Bob Lindahl came bustling toward her on his short, stubby legs. He looked like a cartoon character with his red-and-green plaid trousers and Santa Claus suspenders stretched tightly over his beer belly. Years ago, he'd been a police officer with Danny, and she'd known Bob since she was a little girl. He rested his hand on her shoulder and said, "It's time for you to bring out the cakes, Rue."

"Yes, sir."

"Sir?" His heavy eyebrows lifted. "You used to call me Uncle Bob when me and Danny would take you to the park. Don't you remember the Tickle Monster?"

"Oh, yes." Moisture from his sweaty palm soaked through her white cotton shirt. The way he leered made her glad that she was wearing loose-fitting black slacks and a long apron that disguised her figure.

He chuckled. "I used to tickle you until you screamed for me to stop."

A memory she didn't want to dwell on. When she was a kid, she'd sensed that Bob was a jerk. As an adult, she was sure of it.

Stepping away from his grasp, she said, "I'll get the cakes."

"Need some help?"

Actually, she did. These two cakes were huge and heavy. One was three tiers iced in fluffy white chocolate and decorated with green holly and red berries. The other was a gluten-free, low-fat almond sheet cake. She called the recipe "Ruth-less" because it was lower in calories. The design on top featured the front range of the Rockies surrounding the words: Congratulations, Danny.

"I could use a hand." But she wasn't going anywhere alone with Uncle Bob. "We'll need two more helpers."

He signaled to a muscular guy in sunglasses who stood nearby. Bob introduced him as Carlos. When he leaned forward to shake her hand, Rue glimpsed a shoulder holster under his sports jacket. Obviously a bodyguard.

As they exited the ballroom and went through the kitchen, Bob roped in another volunteer. Rue vaguely remembered him as someone she'd known in high school—a football player who now worked as a foreman at one of Bob's construction sites. His name was Tyler—Tyler Zubek.

Bob reminisced. "Rue used to wear her hair in two braids. Still keeping it long, huh?"

When he reached toward her ponytail, Rue took a couple of quick steps forward. His groping hand clutched nothing but air.

"She was a tomboy," he said to the other two men. "I never thought our little Rue would end up being something feminine like a baker."

If she'd cared about his opinion, she would have run through her credentials: an MBA, culinary school, training as a dessert chef and an apprenticeship with a master baker. She would have talked about the scientific methods she used for testing new ingredients for her cakes and the skilled effort she put into her custom creations.

Instead, she said nothing and left the kitchen. In spite of the season, the weather was un-Christmasy. Though the leaves were off the trees, the temperature had been in the sixties without a hint of snow.

She hurried the rest of the way to her burgundy van, parked in the driveway close to the four-car garage. Uncle Bob's sprawling Colonial redbrick mansion was the only house on this cul-de-sac.

She turned to her helpers. "It'll take two of us to carry each cake. It might be kind of tricky to get them through the kitchen."

She swung open the van door. The three-tier cake

was fantastic with swirls of icing and crystalized sugar snowflakes. Also heavy. And unwieldy.

"Bob and Carlos," she said. "You get this one."

While Rue gave instructions, they removed the cake from the van. The three-foot-long sheet cake was easier for Rue and her former classmate to handle.

From the corner of her eye, she saw someone approaching from the street. A man in a dark sweatshirt with the hood pulled up. There was something odd about his face; his nose was a strange color. And he wore sunglasses.

Carlos saw him, too. He growled, "This is a private party."

"Not anymore."

Still balancing the cake tray in his left hand, Carlos reached inside his jacket for his gun. The three-tier cake teetered wildly.

"What's going on?" Bob demanded. "Who the hell are you?"

She looked over her shoulder. The man in the sweatshirt held a pistol. He fired once, and Carlos went down. The cake fell with a splat.

With a strength borne of panic, Rue whipped her end of the tray from her classmate's hands and hurled it at the gunman. Globs of frosting went flying. Crumbs scattered.

Undeterred, the gunman fired three more times. Three bullets meant for Bob Lindahl. Uncle Bob toppled to his knees. His mouth gaped. His chest was covered in blood.

Rue heard herself scream as she dove for the pavement. Her classmate was right beside her.

The gunman dropped his weapon, pivoted and ran.

Carlos attempted to get up but fell again. His left trouser leg was bloody where he'd been shot. He shoved his gun toward her. "Get him."

Rue knew how to shoot. Danny had taught her. But she had never dreamed of taking aim on another human being. Still, she picked up the gun. Hunched over, she ran to the end of the long driveway. The cul-de-sac was packed with parked cars. Earlier, there had been two young men running a valet service, but they were nowhere to be seen.

She glimpsed the man in the sweatshirt climbing into a car parked half a block away.

She lifted the gun. There was no one else in sight. No one she might hit if a bullet went astray. Could she really do this? Shoot at someone else?

From the back of her mind, she heard a voice. Danny's voice. When she was a kid, she'd been so proud of him. *He was a policeman. Sometimes he had to use his gun to fight the bad guys.*

She had to stop the bad guy. It was up to her. Bracing the gun in both hands, she fired. The blast echoed inside her head. The gun kicked back in her hands. She aimed at the tires and fired again.

Chapter Two

Cody was standing near the door when he heard the commotion out front. Gunshots? He dropped the gym bag holding the Santa outfit and went outside onto the long porch that stretched across the front of the house behind six white pillars.

Other people were pointing, shouting, reacting with varying degrees of panic. Their focus was Rue Harris. She stood in the street, with a gun in her fist. When she gestured helplessly and waved the gun, a woman standing beside Cody shrieked in terror.

To his left, he saw several people gathered beside the maroon van with the Ruth Ann's Cakes logo. Someone was yelling for help. He saw Bob Lindahl's legs in red and green plaid trousers lying on the pavement. What the hell had Rue done?

She took a step toward the house. The people around him gasped and ducked behind the pillars on the wide verandah. Cowards and imbeciles. Couldn't they see she was in shock? Her legs wobbled. She could barely stand.

He went toward her.

"Rue." He spoke her name loudly. Her eyes were glassy and dazed. "Rue, are you all right?"

She nodded.

"Give me the gun."

Eagerly, she held out the black automatic. He took it from her and gathered her into his arms. Her cheek rested against his chest. He could feel her trembling, delicate as a butterfly. "Don't pass out," he said.

"I need to sit down."

With his arm around her shoulders, he guided her back toward the house. The crowd parted before them. From far away, he heard the siren of an ambulance.

When they reached the three steps leading up to the pillared verandah, she sank down onto the stair and leaned forward with her elbows on her knees. Her head drooped.

He sat beside her, arm around her shoulder. "Where did you get the gun, Rue?"

"Carlos the bodyguard." Her voice was barely audible. "He was shot in the leg. The bad man was getting away. I tried to stop him. I tried."

"Everything is going to be okay," he reassured her.

"It's not." She stiffened. "Uncle Bob was shot in the chest. Three times."

Sounded like an assassination. Cody wasn't sure how the murder fit into his own personal agenda, but it couldn't be a coincidence. He was meant to be here. At this particular time. In this particular place.

One of the uniformed officers from the party came up beside them, and Cody handed over the gun.

The officer said, "I'm taking this lady into custody."

"Give us a minute," Cody said. "This is Danny's stepdaughter."

"Oh." The officer took a step back but stayed close, watching in case Rue decided to make a run for it.

Not much chance of that. She was limp, boneless.

Cody held her protectively and watched as another cop, the assistant chief of police, took charge of the scene on the lawn, herding people back into the house and making room for the ambulance.

Rue looked up at Cody. Strands of her wavy brown hair had fallen loose from her ponytail and framed her face. Her complexion was as white as her blood-spattered shirt, but she seemed more controlled. "Why are you helping me?"

A damn good question. Even though he'd decided Rue might be useful to him, that didn't mean he had to come to her rescue. He shrugged. "Somebody had to step up before you shot yourself in the foot."

"Do you think Bob Lindahl will be all right? I've never seen anything like…" Her words trailed off, and she covered her face with her hands.

A light vanilla scent rose from her silky hair. She was sweet and quirky—very different from the perfectly packaged women he usually dated. Those ladies wore the right clothes, knew the right people and said the right things. Not one of them would have been caught dead at a social event waving a gun.

Fighting for composure, she looked toward him again. "I really screwed up."

"What happened?"

"We came out to get the cakes from my van. It was me, Bob and his bodyguard, Carlos. And another guy. His name is Tyler Zubek. We had the cakes in our hands."

She pantomimed holding a tray. "Then this guy started shooting at us. God, it was loud. The only defense I could come up with was to throw my cake at him."

Cody bit the inside of his cheek to keep from laughing out loud. She tried to fight off a gunman with a cake?

"It was a beautiful sheet cake," she said. "A low-fat, gluten-free recipe."

"It's good to know you didn't throw anything fattening."

"But both of my cakes are ruined." A tear slipped down her cheek. "Oh my God, what am I saying? How can I even think about cake? Bob Lindahl might be dead."

He heard the rising panic in her voice and tried to reassure her. "It's okay. You did everything you could."

"Danny is going to be so disappointed in me. I didn't even get the license plate on the getaway car."

Her former stepfather. Danny Mason. He was the reason Cody had come to this party.

Shortly after Danny was elected mayor, Cody had received a manila envelope marked Personal and

Confidential. Inside was a green shamrock tiepin, similar to the one his father had been wearing on the day he'd died. There was also a folded bumper sticker in red, white and blue that said, Danny Mason— Building a Better Denver. The implication? Danny knew something about his father's murder. Cody intended to follow this lead.

Going to the police was a waste of time. They didn't have the manpower to reopen a twenty-year-old case. Nor could Cody march up to the new mayor and start asking pointed questions.

When Rue had introduced herself, he'd seen his opportunity. If he got closer to her, he'd get closer to Danny.

Her eyebrows pinched in a frown. "The gunman did the strangest thing after he shot Bob. He dropped his weapon. Just left it there. Why would he do that?"

"I don't know."

The ambulance arrived and two paramedics raced toward her van. He gave her arm a squeeze and helped her to her feet. "I think we should have the EMTs take a look at you."

"I didn't hurt myself," she protested. "I know how to handle a weapon. Danny taught me."

Speaking of the devil, Danny Mason was coming toward them. In spite of the chill, the sleeves of his green shirt were rolled up to the elbow. He had the forearms of a bricklayer. Or a boxer. If Cody remembered correctly, Danny had once been a Golden Gloves middleweight contender, and he'd stayed in shape. His dark-red hair swept back from a concerned forehead. Though his focus was on Rue, his gaze darted, taking in every detail. He might be mayor, but his cop instincts were still in force.

As he folded Rue into an embrace, he scowled at Cody. "I didn't know you two were friends."

"We just met." Cody wasn't intimidated. "I intend to see more of your former stepdaughter."

"Is that so?"

"Dinner on Saturday." Cody named the most romantic restaurant he could think of. "Chez Mona."

Rue turned her head toward him. "I've been dying to go there. They have a new chef."

"I've met him."

She wriggled out of Danny's embrace and came back toward Cody. "If I could get Chez Mona to serve some of my pastries, my business would take off."

"I can't make any promises," he said. "We'll talk to the chef."

"Hey," Danny interrupted. Like all politicians, he hated being ignored. "This isn't a dating service."

"I know," Rue said crisply. "I was almost killed."

"That's not the way I heard the story," Danny said. "You chased after the shooter. Damn it, Rue. What the hell were you thinking?"

"I did what I thought was right." She stood up straighter, stretching her height to maybe five feet, four inches. "It's like you always used to tell me. Sometimes you have to use your weapon to fight the bad guys."

She must have touched a nerve because Danny looked surprised. "Did I say that?"

"Frequently," she assured him. "You always told me to aim at the midsection. The largest target."

Though she looked as innocent as a newborn fawn, she didn't seem to have any trouble standing up for herself. Cody was beginning to be intrigued by this sweet little cake-baker with a backbone of tempered steel.

A second ambulance parked at the end of the driveway as the first team finished loading Carlos the bodyguard into the rear and pulled away.

"Will Carlos be all right?" she asked.

"Should be." Danny squinted after the ambulance. "One bullet to the thigh."

"And Mr. Lindahl? Is he…"

"Dead," Danny said. "It was fast. There was nothing you could have done to save him."

"Three bullets in the chest," Cody said. "Sounds like a professional hit."

"Let's leave the investigating up to the police," Danny said coldly. "Thanks for keeping an eye on my stepdaughter. I'll take it from here."

Cody wouldn't allow himself to be so easily brushed aside. Rue was his ticket to the inner circle, and he wasn't going to let her get away. "It's no problem," he said as he took her arm. "I'll be happy to escort you over to the ambulance so the EMTs can take a look at you."

"Really," she said. "I'm fine."

"You're shivering like a leaf in the wind." He turned up the charm. With a smile calculated to melt butter, he leaned close and whispered, "Let me take care of you."

Though he recognized suspicion in her gaze, she was too disoriented to object. She trusted him to walk toward the ambulance. Later, she might trust him enough to tell him the family secrets.

TWO HOURS LATER Rue stood alone at the window of a professionally decorated parlor and looked out at the cul-de-sac in front of Bob Lindahl's house. It was almost five o'clock, and the sun had begun its descent behind the mountains. Streaks of gold colored the sky and glimmered on the faded lawn and shrubs. The bare branches of a honey locust danced in the winter breeze. If there hadn't been five police cars and a television van parked farther down the street, this view might have been serene.

Most of the other cars were gone. The guests had been interviewed and sent home. The caterer and his crew had packed up and left. She hadn't seen Cody Berringer leave, and she found herself hoping that he was still here.

Though she had no explanation for why he was so concerned about her, she liked his attention. Who wouldn't? With his black hair and blue eyes, he was every woman's dream date. Protecting her seemed to come naturally to him.

With her fingers, she twirled a long curl. Her hair

hung loose past her shoulders. After the paramedics had checked her out, she'd run a brush through her hair and splashed water on her face. Though she'd taken off her burgundy apron, she still wore the bloodstained white blouse and black slacks.

Repeatedly, Rue had spoken to various homicide detectives and given her story so many times that the sequence of events was permanently imprinted in her brain. The image that stuck with her was Uncle Bob on his knees with his chest covered in blood.

Danny told her that one of the bullets had punctured his heart. A direct hit. He also told her that the gunman had gotten away without a trace—except for the murder weapon, which he so thoughtfully had left behind.

The door to the parlor opened and Danny stepped inside. He had his campaign manager with him. Jerome Samuels was an athletic-looking blond guy in his thirties whom she'd known since childhood. Politically savvy and ambitious, Jerome was looking forward to being appointed to an important position when Danny took the oath of office.

He gave her a calculated but friendly grin. "You ought to be able to leave in just a few minutes."

"Good."

"Here's the deal," Danny said. "I want you to come home with me, Rue."

"Why?"

"Bob Lindahl's murder looks like a professional hit, and you're a witness." Danny never sugarcoated the truth. "Somebody might come after you."

"I can't identify him. He wore sunglasses and the hood of his sweatshirt was pulled up. I didn't even see his hair color."

"You shouldn't be alone," Danny said. "I have plenty of security at my house."

There was also a new wife and her young children from a previous marriage who wouldn't be thrilled to have Rue as a guest. "I have to work," she said.

"Someone else can do it."

"No way. I make custom cakes. They're unique." Her business was brand-new, and she had a reputation to build. "I have to decorate these cakes myself."

"You're being unreasonable."

"Nothing new about that," Jerome added.

Usually, she didn't mind Jerome's teasing, but he'd changed, taken on an air of self-importance that matched his designer suit and solid-gold wristwatch. Plus she was in no mood to be pushed around. "I'm going home to my house. And that's final."

"Think again," Jerome advised.

"My mind is made up, *Jerry.*"

He hated being called Jerry. His full name— Jerome—had dignity. Jerry was a cartoon character. His upper lip curled in disgust. "You sound like your mother, Ruth Ann."

Low blow. Her mother had called three times and was on her way here. "Not even close, *Jerry.* But you might want to brace yourself."

"Why?"

"She's on her way. Ought to be here any minute."

She turned toward the window again and looked out as a familiar car pulled up and parked. The driver's-side door flung open and a well-dressed woman burst out. "Speak of the devil. It's Mom."

"Your mother?" Danny's voice sounded as if his lungs were being squeezed in a vise. He turned to Jerome. "See if you can stop her."

Attempting to control Rue's mother was like commanding a hurricane to turn the other way. She didn't envy Jerome.

"She's not going to listen to me," he said.

He was well-acquainted with Leticia Grant-Harris-Mason-Lopez-Jones-Wyndemere. Adding to his woes, Rue said, "She's married to a judge now. If she doesn't get what she wants, she'll take you to court."

"Aw, hell," Danny muttered. "Might as well get this over with. Come with me, Rue."

They left the parlor and went down the hallway to a grand foyer with marble floors, a sweeping staircase and an ornate crystal chandelier. A couple of the plain-clothes detectives were talking to Cody Berringer. As soon as Cody spotted her, he moved to her side.

In spite of everything that was going on—the cops, the danger, the murder—Cody's nearness ignited a happy little spark inside her. When he took her hand, the flicker became a warm glow.

The front door swung open and her mother stalked inside. Her blond-streaked hair swept back from her forehead. Her crimson silk blouse and black wool suit outlined a slender, expensively maintained figure. She went directly to Danny and confronted him. "I told Ruth Ann that it was a mistake to bake cakes for your party."

"It should have been a good opportunity," Danny said.

"Nothing good ever came from Bob Lindahl." Her blue eyes scanned the opulent foyer. "Although I've got to admit that this house is impressive."

Rue could almost hear the cash register in her mother's head ringing up the cost of the chandelier and the oil paintings on the walls. Leticia had a sensible appreciation for the bottom line.

She held out her arms. "Oh, Ruth Ann. If anything had happened to you—" Her voice choked off. Her eyes welled. Tears? That was so out of character. Her mother never cried.

Leticia pulled her into a ferocious embrace that went on long enough for Rue to begin to feel a little uncomfortable. Then Leticia held her at arm's length, studied her and frowned. "Is that blood on your sleeves?"

"It's not mine."

"Why are you still wearing that shirt?" She swung back toward Danny. "Couldn't you find her some clean clothing?"

Cody stepped forward. "You're right, Mrs. Wyndemere. Rue needs to get home and change clothes. She's had one hell of a rough day."

Leticia surveyed him from head to toe. "Who are you?"

"Cody Berringer."

As he shook her hand, she said, "I've heard of *you*. You work at T&T. Taylor and Tomlinson."

"That's correct."

"A very successful firm," she said.

Rue wasn't in the least bit surprised that her mother knew of Cody. Leticia had an encyclopedic knowledge of Denver's social scene. It was part of her job as a wedding planner—a skill she'd developed when planning her own five marriages.

"And you're Judge Wyndemere's wife," Cody said.

"Small world." The barest hint of a smile touched her mother's lips. "How do you know Ruth Ann?"

"We're going to dinner on Saturday. At Chez Mona."

Hoping to head off any questions about how long she'd been dating Cody, Rue said, "I'm tired. I'd like to leave now."

"Are you sure you're all right?"

"I'm fine, Mom. This is nobody's fault. I just happened to be in the wrong place at the wrong time."

"The wrong place." Leticia shot another glare at Danny. "What kind of mayor are you going to be? You can't even keep your own stepdaughter safe."

"We had plenty of security at this event. Bodyguards. Four of the top cops in the city."

"And a lot of good it did." She jabbed an accusing finger. "You and Bob used to always get into trouble together. And your other cop buddy, Mike Blanco. Oh, I remember—you called yourselves the three amigos. The three stooges is more like it."

Rue tightened her grip on her mother's hand, hoping to rein her in. "It's okay, Mom. Calm down."

"I'm taking you home with me, Ruth Ann."

Danny cleared his throat. "It's best if she comes with me. I have better security at my house."

"Why does she need security? Is she in danger?"

Before they could get into a discussion of professional hit men, Rue said, "I'm *not* going home with you, Mom. Or with Danny. I have my own place."

"Half a duplex in the middle of town," her mother said disparagingly. "Crime central."

"Is it? I never saw anybody killed until I came out here to the suburbs." She looked toward the homicide detective who stood near the door. "Are we done here?"

The detective nodded. "I'll be in touch. We need to schedule a time for you to look through mug shots."

It went without saying that she'd do anything to help their investigation. "I'll call first thing in the morning."

"There's one more thing," the detective said. "Don't talk to the media. We need to control the flow of information."

She nodded. "Do you have the keys to my van?"

"I'm sorry, Miss. Forensics is still going over your vehicle. There might be trace evidence."

Swell. "That kind of leaves me stranded, Detective."

Cody stepped forward. "I'll give you a ride."

My hero. Once again, he was coming to her rescue. "Thank you."

She'd go home, get a good night's sleep and try to forget that she'd had a front-row seat at a professional assassination. She wanted to banish the image of Bob Lindahl, bloody and dying, into the dark recesses of her mind where she locked away all her other bad memories—all those things that were better left unsaid.

Chapter Three

Rue leaned back against the smooth leather seat in Cody's Mercedes sedan. Compared to the way she bounced along in her cake van, this was like riding on a thick, luxurious, heavenly cloud. If that were true, then Cody must be an angel. *Yeah, right.*

She wasn't that naive. Though she hadn't figured out why Cody was being so attentive to her, there had to be an ulterior motive.

Her gaze slid to the left, and she studied him. His dark-gray suit jacket fitted perfectly. On the cuff of his white shirt, she saw a monogram. These were expensive clothes, tailor-made. Definitely not the flowing robes of an angel.

And he was devilishly handsome. Shadows outlined his cheekbones and chiseled jawline. A lock of black hair fell across his forehead.

He adjusted one of the dials on the dashboard. "Warm enough for you? Should I turn up the heat?"

"It's fine." She'd slipped on her black suede jacket over her shirt and slacks. "Nice wheels."

"Six years old and still running like a charm. One of my brothers is a mechanic."

"One of them?" And he'd already mentioned a sister. "How many kids in your family?"

"Five. Three boys and two girls. And I've already got six, no, seven nephews and nieces. I'm the oldest."

"Figures. You act like a big brother."

"How's that?"

"Bossy."

"My brothers and sisters would probably agree with you," he said. "How many siblings do you have?"

She'd need a calculator to figure out the complexities of her many blended families. There were stepbrothers and stepsisters and other children—like Danny's new stepchildren. Did they count as relations? "Genetically, I'm my mother's only child."

"Lucky."

Though his grin probably wasn't meant to be sexy, the curve of his mouth elevated her core temperature. God help her, she wanted to kiss him.

To keep herself from grabbing his shoulders and planting a big wet one on his sexy mouth, she laced her fingers in her lap. "Just in case Danny is right and there's a professional hit man after me, how's this Mercedes in a high-speed chase?"

"Might be fun to find out."

"You probably won't get a chance tonight." She glanced over her shoulder through the back window. A police cruiser was following them to her duplex in the heart of Denver. "We've got a cop escort."

"When are they bringing your van?"

"Tomorrow." Not having transportation was inconvenient but manageable. "It's only five blocks from my house to the shop. I can walk."

"Not alone." His clipped tone indicated his disapproval. "That's a real bad idea."

"Oh, please. I'm not really in danger."

"You don't *want* to believe anything bad is going to happen," he said. "Always hoping for the best. The eternal optimist."

"There's nothing wrong with being positive. What's the alternative?"

"Thinking clearly." At a stoplight, he turned toward her. "Seriously, Rue. Look at the facts."

"Fine," she said. "Even if that alleged professional hit man intends to come after me, how would he know where to find me? How would he know who I am?"

"You were wearing an apron with Ruth Ann's Cakes written across the front. Kind of a big clue."

"True, but—"

"You chased after him," he pointed out. "You fired a gun at his car."

"Okay, he might be ticked off, but—"

"We're talking about a stone-cold killer. Somebody who placed a direct shot in the victim's heart. Somebody you don't take risks with."

Unfortunately, everything he said made sense. He concluded with, "Therefore, you shouldn't be alone tonight."

"Maybe not." But she couldn't bring herself to stay at Danny's house where she'd be an unwanted intruder with his new family. And her mother lived forty minutes away from her shop—time that Rue didn't want to spend commuting back and forth.

She directed him the last few blocks through the older part of Denver near St. Luke's Hospital. In this up-and-coming neighborhood, several of the old mansions had been refurbished as offices, apartments or condos. There was a pride in ownership. Many houses were already decorated with Christmas lights. The four-story condo building on the corner had a neon sleigh and reindeer above the entrance. She pointed out her home, and he parked.

The streetlight reflected off her front window. Two crab apple trees marked the property line between her one-story, blond-brick duplex and the house next door.

As soon as she stepped onto the curb, the two uniformed officers from the cruiser that had followed them came toward her. Their hands rested on the holsters clipped to their belts. "We'll accompany you."

"Thank you," she said. "But you don't have to kick the door down or anything. I have a key."

Surrounded by two of Denver's finest and tall, broad-shouldered Cody Berringer, Rue should have felt safe. But she sensed danger. Could almost smell it. It was like something left too long on the burner.

The exterior of her house looked the same as when she'd left this morning at dawn to work on the cakes for Danny's party. She'd cranked open the miniblinds on the front window so her houseplants would get some sun, and they were still open. No lights shone from the inside.

On the porch, she realized she wouldn't need her key. The red-painted door was ajar. Her home had been broken into. Her premonition of danger became reality.

A jolt of fear hyped up her senses. Behind the trunk of the crab apple tree, she saw a hiding place for a man with a gun. The wind through the shrubs whispered a warning. The rush of traffic from Eighteenth Street sounded like an approaching army.

The two officers reacted immediately. One on each side, they rushed her to their patrol cruiser and shoved her into the backseat. Cody was beside her.

"What's happening?" Her voice trembled.

"They're making sure you're safe," Cody said as he wrapped a comforting arm around her shoulders. "Calling for backup before they enter the house."

She clung to the unraveling threads of her self-control. Already today, she'd fallen apart in this man's arms. *Not again. Damn it, not again.* She wanted to touch him, but not like this. Not in fear. "This isn't fair. Why is this happening to me?"

"You said it yourself, Rue. You were in the wrong place at the wrong time."

Police sirens converged on her neighborhood. *Her home!* Two more patrol cars pulled up at the curb. The officers poured out, guns drawn. It was like watching an action-adventure movie from inside the screen.

She swallowed her fear. "I guess this settles it. I won't be staying at my house tonight."

"Where will you go?"

No idea. There were friends she could call. And people who worked at her shop. But the break-in meant somebody really was after her, and she didn't want to put a friend in danger. "I could get a motel room."

Very gently, he touched her chin and turned her face toward him. "Come home with me."

Her first instinct was to throw herself into his arms and shower him with grateful kisses. But the sane part of her mind objected. She barely knew Cody. "I couldn't."

"I live in a high-rise with a twenty-four-hour-a-day doorman and surveillance cameras. *And* I have an extra bedroom. *And* it's not far from here."

She didn't understand his motivations. He'd already gone well beyond polite support. He was acting as if he really cared about her. "Why are you being so nice?"

"Call it the Christmas spirit."

"Thank you." She might regret this later, but right now, staying with Cody sounded like the best alternative. "And when this is over, I'm going to bake you such a huge cake. Big enough for your whole family."

"Not the low-fat recipe," he said.

"Pure cream and butter and imported chocolate."

On the street, a swarm of uniforms approached her front door. She saw an officer escort the people who lived in the other half of the duplex, a young

African-American couple, to safety. She owed them a cake, too.

If she dumped enough sugar and flour on this situation, it would have to get better.

As HE UNLOCKED the door to his seventeenth-floor condo, Cody wondered if he'd gone too far in offering to let her stay at his place. Asking her for a date had been an expedient means to an end— getting close to Danny. That should have been enough. Instead, he'd waited until she was done with her police interviews. Then he'd driven her home. Now she was here at his condo. Step by step, he was proceeding down a path that wasn't part of his agenda.

The honest truth—something he tried to consider as little as possible—was that he liked being with her. She was quirky and made unexpected moves. Her lack of polish was refreshing.

She dropped her overnight bag and walked across the carpet into the sunken living room, then skipped up the stair to the wall of windows overlooking the lights of Denver and the mountains beyond.

"The penthouse," she said. "Classy."

In spite of everything that had happened to her in the past hours, she beamed a wide grin. Most women would be fearful and traumatized, but not Rue.

"You're handling this well," he said.

"No point in dwelling on something that can't be fixed."

"Your house was trashed. And you're not scared?"

"When you grow up like I did, moving around and changing families, you learn how to keep your problems to yourself."

She sure as hell didn't look like a woman of mystery, but she was an enigma. He wanted to know her secrets and to find out what made her tick.

"Can I get you something to drink?" he asked. "Water? Herbal tea?"

"Vodka with a splash of juice. Any kind of juice."

Again, unexpected.

She followed him into the kitchen where she gushed over his double-sided refrigerator, inspected the inside of the oven and told him exactly how his top-of-the-line appliances were capable of performing.

He prepared the same drink for himself and handed her a tumbler with vodka, ice and orange juice. He held up his glass in a toast. "Here's to better luck."

"Being in the *right* place at the *right* time."

When he gazed into her greenish-blue eyes, he saw a glimmer of sensuality. She tossed her head, sending a ripple through her long chestnut hair. Those thick strands would slip through his fingers like the finest silk.

A warmth generated between them. Not cozy or comfortable, this was a purely sensual heat. Acting on this urge would be insanity. He wasn't really dating Rue and wasn't looking for a relationship. He didn't want to lead her on.

Turning away from her, he set his drink on the

polished granite countertop that separated his kitchen from the living room.

"I feel safe here," she said.

"Good."

"But I'm still angry." Her tone sharpened, reminding him of her mother. "I want the guy who did this to suffer."

"I don't blame you."

The damage at her house had been mostly malicious—obviously meant as a warning. The intruder had slashed the cushions on her flowered sofa, had pulled books off the shelves and had broken all kinds of glassware. Her closets and drawers had been emptied into a pile on the floor. Some of the fabrics were torn. She'd been lucky to find the long-sleeved T-shirt and a pair of jeans that she'd changed into, along with a few other things.

"That creep touched my clothes," she said. "Even this shirt I have on. I want to burn every stitch so I won't be reminded. He stabbed my sofa. And you want to know the worst part? The very worst? He used my chef's knives to do it."

"Why is that so bad?"

"I use those knives for cooking. Baking cakes is my favorite thing, but I love all kinds of cooking, from vegetarian quiche to rack of lamb. I'll never be able to touch those knives without thinking of him. Some faceless man in a hooded sweatshirt. A murderer."

"He won't get away with it. You saw how fast the

cops responded. Every officer in Denver is after this guy."

"Which doesn't mean he'll be caught."

Cody knew from experience that was a true statement. His father's killer had never been apprehended. In spite of the efforts of the police, their only viable suspect had an airtight alibi.

Her eyes blazed as she looked up at him. "I don't ever want to go back to my house again. I just want to move."

"I know people who specialize in cleaning up after crime scenes. I could contact them."

"Great idea." Her anger was replaced by another strong emotion as she took a step toward him. "Thank you, Cody. For everything."

Now was the time for him to back away. But her gaze pulled him closer. She reached up and placed her hand on his shoulder and pulled him toward her for a kiss.

Unexpected. The soft pressure of her lips punched through his nervous system like a hard right jab to the chin. She knocked him out.

Her contented moan resonated inside him. The tips of her breasts grazed his chest as she arched toward him on tiptoe.

Then, she stepped back. When she raised her glass to sip her drink, the ice cubes rattled. Her hand shook, but her eyes were bold. Her cheeks were flushed with a rosy pink.

A tense silence swirled around them. If he didn't

figure out what to say, he'd be tempted to carry her off to his bed. "Are you hungry?"

"Starved." In that single word was a burst of relief. She went into action, opening and closing kitchen cabinets. "I'll whip something up. After all I've put you through today, you deserve dinner."

He wanted more than food. The taste of her lingered and aroused him. But he didn't want to mislead her. He liked her too much.

As she rummaged through his refrigerator, the phone rang and Cody picked up. It was Danny.

"I heard what happened at Rue's house," he said.

And he had probably also heard that she'd gone home with him. "Do you want to talk to her?"

"I called for you, Cody."

He carried the phone into the other room. "Go on."

"First off," Danny said, "I want to thank you for taking care of Rue. She's a great kid."

Not exactly. Rue was a grown woman who didn't need or want her former stepfather hovering over her. "Is there something else you wanted to tell me, Danny?"

"The chief of police has been keeping me in-formed on their investigation. There's something you should know."

"Yes, sir?"

"After Bob was shot, the killer dropped his weapon. He just left it there for us to find."

Cody had no idea why Danny was telling him this. He wasn't an investigator and he didn't handle murder cases. He practiced corporate law. In his negotiations, the only blood that was spilled was symbolic.

Danny continued, "The forensic people have run ballistics tests on the gun."

"Already?"

"Top-priority case."

Of course, it would be. Danny Mason was the newly elected mayor of Denver. Cody waited for him to continue.

"The gun," Danny said. "It was the same weapon used twenty years ago to murder your father."

Chapter Four

In spite of the top-of-the-line appliances, Rue didn't find much in Cody's kitchen that could be turned into an actual meal. A couple of eggs, some dairy creamer and butter. Flour and sugar. Frozen veggies but nothing fresh. Canned soups.

She assembled ingredients and glanced across the granite counter toward the front room where Cody stood at the window, staring down at the city lights. Slowly, he lowered the telephone receiver from his ear. He looked good from the back; his tailored suit coat tapered from his shoulders to his lean torso.

Had she really kissed him? Even though she could still feel the tingling rush of pheromones, she couldn't believe she'd been so impetuous. Could she blame her lack of inhibition on the vodka? Not really. She'd only had a couple of sips. Maybe she wasn't thinking rationally because she hadn't eaten since two o'clock, and it was almost ten.

Instead of joining her in the kitchen, he left the

living room and disappeared down the hall. A little rude, but guys didn't usually announce their trips to the bathroom.

Using a whisk, she whipped up a thin batter for crepes. The process of cooking relaxed her. The smells, flavors and textures of food allowed her to set aside the horrifying events of the day and concentrate on something normal and comforting. She took a healthy swig of her vodka and orange juice. Cooking was something she did well. Not like relationships.

In her life so far, there had only been one serious attachment. She'd lived with one guy—an archeology major—for three months before he left for a dig site in Peru. They'd intended to get back together, but it didn't work out. And she hadn't been heartbroken. They were compatible but lacked fire.

In her brief kiss with Cody, she'd felt more passion than in her whole time in that other relationship. The intensity was a little bit scary…and a little bit wonderful. She needed to be careful not to get carried away, not to expect too much.

When he returned to the kitchen, he'd changed from his suit to jeans and a faded red University of Denver sweatshirt. The clothes were casual, but he was tense. He took a seat on the opposite side of the granite counter between the kitchen and the living room. His expression dark and brooding, he drained most of his vodka and orange juice in one long gulp.

"Bad phone call?" she asked.

"It was Danny."

And he didn't ask to talk to her? He must be aware that she was staying here. She'd told the lead homicide detective where she could be reached, and he'd certainly report back to her former stepfather. "What did he say?"

"They've already done ballistics on the gun from the crime scene."

"Wow, that was fast."

"Danny has a lot of pull. The murder of Bob Lindahl is the number-one case for the Denver PD."

"Well, that's good news, isn't it?" She found a copper-bottom skillet in a lower cabinet and fired up the gas burner. "The quicker they investigate, the more likely they'll solve the crime. Right?"

"True. My father's body wasn't found for sixteen hours. He lay dead on the concrete floor of a warehouse while the killer covered his tracks."

She heard the bitterness in his voice. "He was an assistant district attorney. I'm sure the police investigated thoroughly."

"Not good enough."

She flipped a smidgen of butter into the skillet and watched it melt. The secret to perfect crepes was having exactly the right heat. "How old were you?"

"Twelve."

The oldest of five children. "It must have been hard on you."

"It was worse for my mother. My parents were one of those couples who were best friends as well as lovers. Always laughing. They couldn't keep their hands off each other. Embarrassing for us kids. But in a good way."

She poured a stream of batter into the skillet. "Did she ever remarry?"

"Didn't even date. She used to say that she'd already had the one true love of her life. Nobody else could live up to her memories of my father."

She wondered if the same was true for Cody. He spoke of his parents' relationship with such reverence. Could it be that he wanted the same thing and wasn't willing to settle for less? That might explain why this very eligible bachelor wasn't married.

Carefully, Rue flipped the crepe. Lightly browned but not crispy. Perfect. She transferred the thin pancake to a plate and poured another. "How hungry are you? Do you want two or three?"

"Don't you want to hear about the ballistics?"

"I doubt it'll mean anything to me. I don't pay much attention to the news, don't even know the names of the current bad guys. Or gangs. Or whatever."

"At one time, you did," he said. "While Danny was your stepfather."

She pulled off another perfect crepe. "He did a lot of work with gangs when I was a kid. That's where I first met Jerome Samuels, his campaign manager. Jerome's father was a gang leader."

"I wasn't aware of that."

"You must be the only one." She poured more batter. "Jerome loves to tell his story. How he was a thug, a gangsta, a juvenile delinquent. Then he pulled himself out of his life of crime, went to college and became a big, fat success."

"Is it true?"

"Mostly," she admitted. "I was just a kid at the time when Danny was involved in gang negotiations, and I resented the attention he gave to anybody else, including Jerome."

"The gang project," Cody said. "That turned into a career move for Danny. His place in those negotiations launched him into politics."

Another endeavor that had taken his focus away from Rue. Even worse, her mother had gotten involved. When Leticia jumped into the political arena and took up networking, she no longer had time for Rue's school plays and field trips. Her mother couldn't wait to make the transition from cop's wife to the spouse of a respected legislator.

As it turned out, the joke was on her. Their marriage disintegrated shortly after Danny was elected as a state representative.

Rue poured the last of the batter into the pan. "Are you going to tell me about the ballistics?"

"The gun used to kill Bob Lindahl was the same weapon that killed my father."

She dropped the spatula and whirled around to face him. "The same gun?"

"A Colt .45 automatic."

No wonder Cody had been tense. He would be forced to confront his father's death as part of the ongoing investigation. She wished for a way to comfort him but knew it would be impossible to console him for his loss. "How does Bob Lindahl's murder connect with your father's?"

"I assume it has something to do with events that happened twenty years ago."

"Lindahl was a cop back then."

"So was Danny."

The hostile edge in Cody's voice disturbed her. "Surely you don't think Danny was involved in your father's murder?"

"They were both investigating the gangs. My father and Danny worked together. They knew each other."

"So?" His insinuations were beginning to tick her off.

"The same weapon that killed my father was used on Lindahl this afternoon at a party for Danny's supporters. Obviously Danny is involved."

"With a murder? Danny's no saint, but there's no way he'd ever have anything to do with murder."

"I'm just saying—"

"Well, don't. Don't even think it."

She glanced back toward the skillet where her last crepe was burning. There was no way to repair that burnt mess. Yanking the skillet off the stove, she scraped the charred remains into the sink.

Cody's suspicion of Danny grated on her nerves. Throughout Danny's mayoral campaign, she'd put up with a lot of innuendo, but that was from journalists looking for dirt. Somebody like Cody ought to know better.

Nonetheless, she shouldn't have snapped at him. He'd had shocking news, wasn't himself. He was upset. But so was she, damn it.

Quickly, she assembled the rest of the ingredients for crepes stuffed with creamed tuna, cheese and vegetables. She'd intended to add an over-easy egg on the side, but her hands were shaking. This was too much stress for one day.

While she set the plates on the glass-topped table in the dining area, Cody refreshed their drinks.

He sat beside her, and they each took a taste. The crepes were okay but not a recipe that would go into her keeper file.

"Not bad," he said.

"I didn't have much to work with."

Less than half an hour ago, she'd kissed him. But that sensual warmth was as chilled as gazpacho. She didn't want to be here. "It might be best if I book myself into a motel tonight."

He glanced up sharply. "I want you to stay."

"I'd rather not impose. You have a lot to think about. The police investigation is going to rake up a lot of memories."

"I welcome the investigation. I want my father's murderer caught. That's all I've ever wanted."

"I should go."

"Stay." He reached over and placed his hand atop hers. "This isn't about me. It's about you."

His touch surprised her, and she pulled her hand

away. His friendliness felt phony. Why did he want her here? What was he after?

"You've had a hell of a day, Rue. What kind of man would I be if I threw you out in the cold?"

An honest one. There was no particular reason he should care about her well-being. "I can take care of myself."

He turned on a smile that was as fake as a plastic ficus. "Stay here and get a good night's sleep. Things will look better in the morning."

She seriously doubted that.

AFTER RUE had gone to bed, Cody went into his home office, leaving the door partially open. If Rue tried to sneak out in the middle of the night, he wanted to be able to hear. At the very least, he was responsible for her safety.

His plan for using her to get closer to Danny was a fiasco. He'd made the mistake of insulting Danny, and loyalty to her former stepfather ran deep. Without hesitation, she'd defended Danny's reputation for being a good guy, a former cop with a sterling reputation.

Cody knew better. *Nobody* was shiny pure. *Everybody* made mistakes, took shortcuts that bordered on illegal, followed their personal interests. *Everybody* had secrets in their past, even the newly elected mayor of Denver.

How could Rue blindly defend him? She was smarter than that. Quick-witted and funny, her mind worked in a relatively logical pattern in spite of the unexpected twists. Like when she'd kissed him.

He sank into the chair behind his desk. That kiss had been one hell of a surprise. He hadn't intended for this relationship to turn sexual. Even a great white shark had enough scruples to know it was wrong to seduce a woman for information. He'd only wanted to be friends with Rue, to get close enough to infiltrate Danny's inner circle.

Instead, his thoughts ranged over her luscious little body, imagining the texture of her skin and the feel of her long, silky hair. Unlike many of the women he dated, Rue wasn't the type who could handle a casual fling. She'd expect more from him, more than he could deliver. Hell, it might be best to say a polite goodbye and forget he'd ever met her.

On the desktop in front of him was a square cardboard box—his Lucky Ted file. Inside were folders with legal documents, copies of his father's death certificate and insurance papers, reports from a private detective, mementos and photographs. He took out a scrapbook he'd started shortly after his father was murdered.

On the beat-up cover was a faded picture of the Rockies, a reminder of camping trips on the Platte River. The pages were filled with Cody's own handwriting—a twelve-year-old's scrawl and newspaper clippings.

The year was 1987. Ronald Reagan was President. The hit movie was *Fatal Attraction*. Michael

Jackson was singing "Bad." Local news focused on Colorado Senator Gary Hart who'd been shot down in his run for the presidency when he'd been caught with his pants down. The New Age community was mobilizing for the harmonic convergence in Chaco Canyon. And Lucky Ted Berringer was shot dead in a Denver warehouse.

Though Cody knew all this information by heart, he scanned the clippings, looking for mentions of Danny Mason.

At the time of his murder, his father had been focusing on an investigation of gang violence and drug dealing which had led to allegations of local cops taking bribes to look the other way on crime. Lucky Ted had gotten a tip from a suspect in a drive-by shooting and was on his way to meet with this informant when he was murdered. A week later, the snitch also turned up dead. It was assumed that both murders were gang-related. Arrests were made, but no one was ever charged.

As he scanned the articles, the name of one of the gang leaders popped out: Jackson Samuels. The father of Jerome Samuels? Rue had mentioned Jerome's juvenile-delinquent background. How old was Jerome at the time of Lucky Ted's murder?

Cody turned on his computer and searched the Internet for a quick bio on Jerome. He was fourteen in 1987, old enough to pull a trigger. His juvenile record was sealed but there were ways of accessing that information. Jerome had gone to the University of Colorado in Boulder on a baseball scholarship and graduated with a degree in political science. After that he'd worked on some political campaigns and spent a couple of years as a lobbyist. Then he became Danny's right-hand man.

Was Jerome Samuels the person who had sent him the campaign bumper sticker for Danny and the shamrock tiepin? If so, why? Jerome wouldn't want to implicate Danny who was about to become mayor and, very likely, appoint Jerome to a high position.

Cody stared at the computer screen. He should have made the connection to Jerome on his own, but it had taken Rue to point it out. She knew the family secrets, and he couldn't let her go until she'd told him everything.

Returning to the past, Cody flipped through old newspaper articles. Danny Mason had been mentioned in the cop scandal, as had Bob Lindahl. And a dozen other Denver cops. In the Internal Affairs investigation, both were cleared of suspicion.

Cody brushed his thumb over a yellowed newspaper clipping with his father's photograph. A familiar wave of sadness washed through him. News reports could only skim the surface; mere words were unable to express how the loss of a father affected a family. Though the Berringers stayed on in the same rambling old house, the halls seemed vacant. His father's seat at the head of the table remained empty until a year and a half later at Thanksgiving when Cody, at age fourteen, took that position to carve the turkey. He had become the man of the house.

His mother hadn't been much help. She'd managed to drag herself through the day in her job as a schoolteacher, but she was exhausted by the time she got home.

He flipped open the lid on a cigar box. The photograph on top was a wedding picture of his father and mother. So young. So hopeful.

A tear slipped down his cheek as he tried to reconcile the pretty, smiling brunette in the wedding photo with the way his mother looked now. She seemed to have faded. Her hair was gray. Her baggy clothes hung on her thin frame.

He heard a sound from the hallway and looked up in time to see Rue's back. Had she been spying on him? Had she seen him cry?

He bolted from the chair. Anger surged through him as he stormed down the hall to the guest bedroom. Why the hell was she sneaking around in here? What was she after? Without knocking, he yanked open the door to the guest bedroom.

She stood in the middle of the room wearing a pink nightshirt—one of the few items of clothing she'd thrown into her overnight bag. Her long hair fell all the way to the tips of her breasts.

"Were you spying on me?" he demanded.

She lifted her chin. "I was looking for you. I wanted to apologize."

"For what?"

"Being rude."

Her hazel eyes were red-rimmed, and her pale cheeks were smudged. She looked as though she might have been crying, herself. Because of something he'd done? Something he'd said? He didn't want to care about her. She was only a means to an end. Danny Mason's little girl.

"How long were you standing in the door to my office?"

"Only a minute. You looked busy, and I didn't want to disturb you."

Cody tried to give her a disarming smile. But he couldn't. Too many sorrows from the past weighed upon him. Past rage. Past frustration.

This was his burden. His alone. He didn't share his past with anyone. Especially not someone from the enemy camp. "There's no need to say you're sorry."

"But I am. You've been really nice to me. All day. I don't know how I would have gotten through all this without your help. I shouldn't have fussed at you. So there. I'm sorry."

He could feel her retreating from him, pulling away. Their budding friendship was dying on the vine. He couldn't have that. He needed her.

Time to turn on the charisma. He was brilliant at charming people. Juries loved him. Women wanted to be with him. Rue would be no different.

He took a step toward her. A kiss should solve everything. He rested his hand on her shoulder. Though he felt her tense, he leaned down.

"What are you doing?" she demanded.

"Showing you that we can be friends."

His hand slid down her arm, and he anchored her in place. His lips were inches away from hers when she pulled away. "Stop it, Cody. This isn't right."

"You kissed me before," he reminded her. He knew that she wanted him. He held her other arm. "Come on, Rue. Lighten up."

She wrenched away from him, drew back her arm and slapped him. Hard. What the hell?

"I'm sorry again," she said, "for hitting you. Now, please leave."

He pivoted and left the room. Getting close to Rue would be harder than he'd thought.

Chapter Five

Early the next morning, Rue was dressed and ready to go before Cody stirred. She was out the door to his condo building and on her way to work when a police cruiser pulled over the curb. They'd been keeping an eye on her, probably hoping that the killer might come after her again and they could nab him.

They gave her a lift, and she arrived at her store-front shop a few minutes before six o'clock. She didn't always come in so early; her assistant, Bernice Layne, was responsible for preparing the fresh pastries and opening at seven. But Rue had a big day scheduled: the creation of a four-tier wedding cake for tomorrow. The bride was of Scottish heritage and the icing design called for the clan tartan to be hand-painted on the edge of each tier.

She unlocked the alley door and slipped inside. The kitchen at Ruth Ann's Cakes was warm and redolent with the smell of cinnamon buns, muffins and blueberry turnovers—delicious scents that usually comforted her. But not today. It was going to take more than a dash of sugar and spice to erase the bad taste Cody had left in her mouth.

Not that he was entirely to blame for her sour mood. Yesterday, she'd witnessed a murder, and that vision wouldn't fade. Though she couldn't remember her dreams, she'd startled awake twice during the night. No matter how hard she tried, she couldn't completely dismiss her fear.

To make matters worse, Rue saw that Bernice was not alone. "Good morning, Mom."

"Hello, dear."

"What are you doing here?"

"It's obvious," she said. "I'm here to help out."

That didn't often happen. Though Rue worked with her mother to coordinate cakes for her wedding planner service, Leticia avoided getting her hands dirty. And she was seldom up and about before noon.

Suspiciously, Rue asked, "Why are you *really* here?"

"I've been worried about you," Leticia said. She linked arms with Bernice. "We've been worried."

As if having one mother wasn't enough? Leticia and Bernice were approximately the same age, both blond, both attractive. Her mother was tasteful and elegant with a single strand of real pearls around her throat. Bernice, a former professional drag queen, never appeared without full makeup. At six o'clock in the morning, her eyes were rimmed with lavender shadow. False eyelashes fluttered. Her lips were neon-pink. While baking, she covered her platinum hair with a beaded hairnet that looked like something a deranged medieval princess might wear. Under her long white apron, she wore a hot-pink Spandex top and tight paisley capris that showed off her shapely dancer's legs.

Of course, taste in clothing wasn't the biggest difference between these two. Bernice was a man.

"You turned off your cell phone," Bernice accused.

"And didn't answer your home phone," her mother added.

Rue glared at both of them. She wasn't in the mood for a guilt duet. "I have nothing to say. Not to either of you."

With a quick pivot, she turned and went into the office where paperwork surrounded her computer in neat stacks. She hung her suede jacket on a peg and slipped an apron over her head. She hated that her mother was here. Helping out? Hah! Leticia was up to something. Just like Cody had a hidden agenda. Why couldn't anybody tell her the truth?

"Rue?" Bernice stood in the doorway. Her pink lips pulled into a concerned frown. "Are you okay, honey?"

"I'm fine."

"I knew last night that something was wrong. The murder was on the ten o'clock news."

She groaned. "What did they say on the news?"

"The cops are on the case. No leads. Blah, blah, blah. When they showed a live feed, they zoomed in on your van and I could read the logo: Ruth Ann's

Cakes." Her long fingers flashed like spotlights. "Wow! Talk about great promo."

"Having my cakes be part of a crime scene?"

"Honey, any publicity is good publicity. At least, that's what they say in showbiz."

From the kitchen, she heard a timer go off. Her mother called out, "What am I supposed to do? The cinnamon rolls will burn to a crisp."

"I'm coming," Bernice shouted. To Rue, she said, "Cut your mother some slack. She really is worried."

Really? Leticia had never been a doting mother, and it was a little too late to start now.

Rue pulled her hair into a bun, then put on her chef's hat. Avoiding her two helpers in the kitchen, she went to the front of the shop behind the sales counter and measured fresh grounds into the coffee container. Typically, they only had a few early-morning walk-ins. Throughout the day, people drifted in—mostly for cookies and brownies. The majority of their business came from custom-made cakes and pies for special occasions.

Thanksgiving had been busy, but they were in a lull. Aside from the tartan wedding cake for tomorrow, there were only two other simple cakes on order for the weekend. She'd been hoping that her specially designed gingerbread houses would catch on for the Christmas season.

When she returned to the kitchen, her mother was carefully arranging muffins on a tray that would go into the front display case. Bernice used a pastry tube to squeeze creamy icing onto the cinnamon rolls.

"You never told us," her mother said. "Why didn't you answer your home phone last night?"

"Because I didn't spend the night at my house." Rue bit her lip. She hadn't intended to tell anybody—least of all, her mother—about Cody. Too late now. Both her mother and Bernice gaped.

"Where did you stay?" Leticia asked.

There was no point in lying. Sooner or later, her mother would weasel out the truth. Rue shrugged. "I spent the night with Cody Berringer."

"A guy?" Bernice squeezed the icing tube extra hard. A glob oozed out. "Is he hot?"

"Tall, dark and handsome. Black hair and blue eyes." She faced her mother. "I didn't sleep with him."

Bernice dropped the icing tube and spread her hands wide. "Why not?"

"That's a terrible question," Leticia said. "Rue didn't sleep with him because she's a good girl. Isn't that right?"

"Yes, Mother." If there was one lesson her frequently married mother tried to teach her, it was not to sleep with a man until you had a marriage contract tucked away in your pocketbook.

Not that Leticia's life story was something Rue wanted to emulate. She explained, "There's nothing going on between me and Cody. He's the most arrogant man I've ever met." Remembered anger tensed in her chest. "I slapped him."

"Juicy," Bernice said. "Tell us more."

"He's not my type. Too dark and brooding. His father was murdered when he was a kid. Lucky Ted Berringer." She turned to her mother. "You must have known him."

"We never met. He was an assistant district attorney. Of course, Danny knew him. The DAs and the police have to work together."

Rue remembered how Cody had tried to turn that logical connection into a sinister accusation. "How well did Danny know him?"

"Enough to be terribly upset by the murder." The barest hint of a frown creased her mother's forehead. "At the time, there was a great deal of gang violence. Drive-by shootings. Carjackings. And then, the police scandal."

This was the first Rue had heard of a scandal. "Based on what?"

"I remember," Bernice chimed in. "That was back in the day. God, it must have been twenty years ago. When I was still performing regularly. A bunch of cops were under investigation for taking bribes and looking the other way on gang business."

"Danny wasn't involved," Leticia said firmly. "But I wasn't so sure about Bob Lindahl."

"Why not?"

"Money."

That was a topic her mother understood very well. "What about money?"

"Cops aren't paid well," Leticia said, "but when

Bob Lindahl left the force to start his construction business, he had the upfront capital. He said it came from loans, but I was never really sure."

"And Cody's father was investigating the bribes?" Rue questioned.

"Mostly, he concentrated on the gangs."

But he could have presented a threat to Bob Lindahl. So there actually was a connection, other than the obvious fact that the same gun was used to kill Cody's father and Uncle Bob.

"Let's get back to the important stuff," Bernice said. "You and this Cody person. If you don't like him, how come you spent the night at his place?"

"I couldn't stay at home. Somebody broke in and trashed the place."

"They're after you?"

"I guess so," Rue said quietly.

"Holy hell!" Bernice gestured extravagantly. "Why didn't you tell us?"

"I just did."

Bernice darted her dramatic eyes back and forth. "When I got here this morning, there was a car parked out front. Maybe it was him. The killer. Rue, honey, he might be out there right now."

The fear she'd swept into a secret corner of her mind burst in a dizzying surge. She could feel the blood draining from her face. Off balance, she braced one hand against the stainless-steel countertop. They were safe in the kitchen. The only windows were eight feet off the floor.

Her gaze lifted toward those high panes of glass, reflecting the thin light of dawn. The metal surfaces of appliances, countertops and sinks gleamed coldly. In spite of the warmth, a chill tightened her lungs. He could be out there. The killer could be on the street, waiting for his chance, waiting to kill her.

Her mother took her hand. "Rue? Are you okay?"

There wasn't much choice. She had a lot to do and couldn't spend the whole day cowering in a corner. In a weak but hopeful voice, she tried to deny the danger. "It's a busy street. There are always cars."

"There was a guy sitting in this one." Bernice stalked into the office where they hung their coats and returned carrying her massive pink purse—a designer knock-off that wasn't fooling anyone. Reaching down to the very bottom, she pulled out a small pistol with a pearl handle.

Rue wasn't entirely surprised. "You're armed."

"I'm a tough cookie. I even have the recipe."

Including walnuts, peanut brittle and dark chocolate chunks. A person could break a tooth on Bernice's tough cookies. But it was a long way from baked goods to bullets. Rue didn't feel reassured. "If that car is still out there, I'll call the police. Where was he parked?"

"By the alley. You stay here and I'll sneak out to the front window and take a peek."

"Good idea," her mother encouraged.

"No sneaking," Rue said. "The display counter is glass and the storefront window is huge. If anybody's out there, they'll see you. I'm calling the police. Right now."

As Rue reached for the phone in the office, it rang. Who could possibly be calling at half past six in the morning? She picked up. "Ruth Ann's Cakes."

"Hi, Ruth Ann. I'm with Channel Two news and I'd like to set up a time when—"

"No comment." She disconnected the call and turned to Bernice and her mother. "A reporter."

"And you hung up?" Her mother was appalled. "Ruth Ann, this is free publicity."

It didn't seem right to take advantage of the situation. "This is about a murder. Bob Lindahl is dead."

"Which is no reason why you can't start taking orders on gingerbread houses for Christmas."

From the front of the shop, the doorknob rattled. Rue gasped. Was it him? The killer?

Bernice edged toward the door and peeked around the edge. "Wow. If he's a murderer, shoot me now."

Rue peered around her and saw Cody at the door, silhouetted against the pink dawn. He hammered on the glass and called out, "Rue, I need to talk to you."

Bernice made a yummy noise. "Is that the guy you spent the night with?"

"That's him." Leticia made the identification. "A very successful lawyer."

"And a classy dresser. Is that a cashmere overcoat?"

"Definitely," Leticia said. "I can spot cashmere from a hundred yards. Go let him in."

"Stop," Rue said. "If you two would stop ogling

for a minute, you might remember that a murderer could be parked at the curb."

"He's not gunning for me," Bernice said. "I'll risk it."

She sashayed to the front door, unlocked it for Cody and locked up again. She waved her gun toward the kitchen. "It's okay. The car is gone."

"What car?" Cody asked. "What's going on?"

Bernice said, "I saw someone lurking outside."

He reached inside his suit coat and pulled out a gun. Rue couldn't believe it. Now there were two armed civilians standing in the front of her shop. Swell. "Would you both please put down your weapons? This is a bakery, not a shooting range."

When Cody strode toward the kitchen with his black cashmere overcoat swirling around him like a cape, he cut an impressive figure. Up close? Even better. The glow from his blue eyes was intoxicating, but she was immune to his charms.

The same wasn't true for Leticia and Bernice who fluttered around him like flies to buttercream icing. Her mother would be thrilled if Rue hooked up with Cody—the handsome, successful, eligible, corporate shark. One of Leticia's oft-repeated bits of maternal wisdom was: It's just as easy to fall in love with a rich man as a poor one. She deftly maneuvered Cody toward Rue and gave them some space.

He was careful not to get too close. In a low voice, he said, "I was concerned about you."

"Didn't you see the note I left by the coffeemaker?"

"A very nice, very formal thank-you."

The phone in the office rang again, and her mother went to answer.

"Last night," Cody said, "didn't turn out the way I expected. I was a jerk."

In her opinion, that was a fair assessment. "Are you trying to tell me that you're sorry?"

"I never apologize."

"Don't like to admit when you're wrong?"

"Assigning blame is a futile and endless exercise. You say you're sorry and I forgive you. Then I do the same." He slipped his gun back into the shoulder holster. "What's the point of going round and round?"

"Clearing the air. Building trust."

What she wanted from him was honesty. She wanted to know his ulterior motives—the real reasons why he'd made a date with her in the first place and why he'd been so supportive.

"There's another reason I came here," he said. "I had a call from a reporter I've worked with. The media is jumping on this story, and they'll want to talk to you."

"A television reporter already called here." She glanced toward the office where her mother was still on the phone. No doubt she was arranging interviews. "There isn't much way to avoid them."

"I'd appreciate if you don't mention the gun."

"I won't," she snapped. "That would be hearsay. Besides, the homicide detective asked me not to talk to the media."

Leticia charged out of the office. "Get ready, folks. Crews from two television stations are going to be here within the hour. If we play this right, we'll be live on the morning news."

"But I promised the police I wouldn't say anything."

"It's all right, dear. Give them a 'no comment' and show them the gingerbread houses."

Bernice was beaming, clearly thrilled. "We're going to need more pastries. Cody, we could use your help."

"I don't think so," Rue said. She wanted Cody gone. It was too confusing to deal with him, the media and the fact that a murderer was after her.

The office phone trilled, and her mother darted back into the office. Bernice headed toward the bathroom. "I've got to fix my hair. There could be photographers."

Rue was left standing in the kitchen with Cody. "I really can't ask you to—"

"I'm volunteering." He peeled off his overcoat and suit jacket. "Where do I start?"

Her pride told her to shove him out the door and forget she'd ever met him. But she had to be practical. Reporters were showing up on her doorstep, and she didn't have enough food. Cody had offered to help, and she needed the extra hands.

"Lose the shoulder holster," she said. "Grab an apron, put on a chef's hat and wash your hands."

Baking came first.

Chapter Six

Rue flushed every other concern from her mind. If Ruth Ann's Cakes was going to appear in the media—even in connection with a homicide—she wanted to show off her shop in the best possible light. They only had half an hour.

After she got Cody started filling muffin cups, she went to the refrigeration unit and pulled out the already baked and decorated gingerbread houses for the front window. Dashing back and forth, she set up the display as a Christmas village with two gingerbread mansions, a church and a small cottage. On each end, she placed a three-tiered snowman cake with curly white-chocolate icing and dark-chocolate button eyes.

In the kitchen, Bernice was showing Cody how to mix and pour pineapple coffee cakes. She waved to Rue. "I called the weekend clerks to come in."

"Good thinking." But Rue was more concerned about the baked goods. Their supply of pastries was barely enough to fill the front case.

She grabbed four already baked pound cakes from the fridge. At the table where she did her icing work, she mixed a citrus-and-vanilla icing to drizzle over the top and garnished them with marzipan shaped like mistletoe.

Glancing up, she caught Cody watching her. He didn't look away. Nor did he flash one of his handsome but insincere smiles. He just gave her a wink—a sign of frank approval that she found a hundred times more charming than his fireworks charisma.

At seven o'clock, when Bernice opened the front door, Rue braced herself for a stampede of reporters and television crews. All she heard were the sounds of Bernice opening the cash register and fussing with the coffeemaker. Breathing hard, she looked at Cody.

He straightened his shoulders and brushed his hands on his apron. His chef's hat fell low on his forehead. The heat from the ovens flushed his complexion. A smudge of flour creased his cheekbone.

"Once again," she said, "you've come to my rescue."

"I know my way around a kitchen," he said. "I had four younger brothers and sisters to cook for."

A timer rang, and he pulled a tray of muffins from the oven. With a shock, she realized that this was a man she could fall in love with. A practical man who didn't mind rolling up his shirtsleeves and getting busy.

She heard the tinkling bell as the door opened. Voices echoed from the front of the shop.

Standing beside Cody, she arranged the fresh

muffins on a display tray. "Bernice was right about the photographers. How do I look?"

"Like a professional baker." He took off her chef's hat and grinned. "You're pretty damn cute."

She sensed that this was the first real compliment he'd given her. His words boosted her confidence. "I know you don't like apologies and the regular courtesies, but it's important for me to say this. Thank you."

He gave a quick nod. "I'll stick around in case you need me."

Carrying the tray of muffins, she left the kitchen and went to the front counter in time to hear Bernice say, "The coffee is free. And so are the pastries."

There were four people. Two of the men wore jackets with the Channel Two logo.

Bernice introduced her like a celebrity and added, "Be sure to check out our display of gingerbread houses in the front window. Perfect for the holidays."

Though Rue tried to hide behind "no comment," the interviewer had already pieced together most of the story, including the part where she threw her cake at the gunman. They must have already talked to Tyler Zubek or Carlos the bodyguard or one of the cops. "Who told you about throwing the cake?"

"A source," the interviewer said. "Is it true?"

Obviously, she wasn't giving up anything that wasn't already common knowledge. Rue nodded.

Her mother dashed up beside her. "You might be interested to know we offer cakes that are low-fat and gluten-free. The recipe is called Ruth-less."

The slender female reporter turned toward her. "Cake that's low in calories?"

"Not dietetic," Rue said quickly. She didn't want to give the impression that she'd discovered a cake that would make you skinny. "But we offer a number of healthy alternatives, using natural sweeteners. Did you notice our Christmas display of gingerbread houses in the window?"

Distracted from the crime, the reporter followed her to the window. Free publicity was a very good thing.

Three more people arrived. Then another two. With expert help from Leticia, the cameramen figured out angles where they could set up their interviews.

Rue found herself backed into a corner by the front window. Instead of talking about the crime, she offered advice on how cakes could be used as edible centerpieces. Framed photographs on the walls showed some of her more spectacular triumphs. A Bon Voyage cake in the shape of the Eiffel Tower. A cherry-red hot rod for a little boy's birthday. A ski slope. A six-tier wedding cake covered entirely in edible yellow roses.

Bernice rushed up to her side, pointed to the curb and whispered in her ear, "That's the car I saw this morning."

Alarmed, Rue glanced outside as a burly man got out of the car. He was too big and too tall to be the killer, but he looked menacing behind his dark glasses. When he pushed open the door to the shop, people gave him room.

He focused on her. "I'm looking for Ruth Ann."

Though she hadn't been aware of Cody's presence, he was beside her. In a cool but dangerous tone, he questioned the thug. "Who are you?"

"Danny hired me. I'm a bodyguard."

Cody nodded his approval. "Let's see some identification."

Rue turned on her heel and retreated into the kitchen. She didn't want to cause a scene with reporters waiting, but she didn't appreciate being put in this position. If Danny intended to hire a bodyguard, he should have checked with her first.

Her mother joined her. "I must say, I'm surprised that Danny is being so thoughtful."

"I don't need a bodyguard."

"I beg to differ, Ruth Ann. Until the police make an arrest, you need protection."

All this attention was too much. Her mother fluttering around her. Reporters asking questions. Danny hiring a bodyguard. Too much. Rue's frayed nerves pulled tighter, and she pressed her lips together to keep from snapping at Leticia. Her mother meant well. They all meant well, but that did nothing to loosen the tension.

Cody came toward her and took her arm. To her mother, he said, "Would you take care of the media for a moment?"

"Gladly." Adjusting her pearls, she returned to the front of the store. "Who wants muffins?"

He escorted Rue into the office and shut the door.

Letting go of her arm, he took a step back. "Go ahead. Say what you're thinking."

"What do you mean?"

"When that guy said he was a bodyguard, you looked like you were going to explode. You're angry."

"You don't know that," she said. "You can't tell what I'm thinking. Why did you drag me in here?"

"You need to vent." He rested a hip on her desk. His arms folded across his chest. "Come on, Rue. Tell me."

"You really want to know? Well, fine. Here's what I'm thinking. Nothing good can come from being the center of attention. Everybody smiles and applauds and then—without warning—it turns bad. They're pointing at you. Seeing all your flaws and your fears."

Though she kept her voice low and controlled, a lifetime of pent-up emotion raged inside her. Growing up, she was always the new kid. Going to a new school. Being part of a new family. An object of curiosity. "I don't want to see my face on the evening news. Don't want to be in the spotlight. Don't need a damn bodyguard."

Instead of criticizing, Cody nodded calmly. He was listening, taking her seriously. Perhaps too seriously.

Wishing she could take her words back, she tried to lighten the mood with a smile, but the muscles in her face wouldn't respond. She blurted, "I learned that it was safer to stay in the background and keep my mouth shut. What you don't say can't hurt you."

"Okay," he said.

She paced a few steps in her crowded office and

threw up her hands. "Now I suppose it's time for you to tell me I should suck it up and accept the body-guard that Danny so kindly hired to protect me."

"You're in danger, Rue. Accept the bodyguard and move on."

"Should I?"

"Hell, yes."

His confidence was the direct opposite of her inse-curity. A natural leader, Cody could easily take control of any situation. And she decided to let him. "All right. I'll keep the bodyguard. Better safe than sorry."

"And I'll arrange for someone to clean your house?"

"Yes, please." She liked the way he brought order to chaos. "While you're at it, would you see if the police are ready to release my van?"

"Consider it done."

His features relaxed. Apparently, he was relieved to finally be in charge. And she was equally glad to relinquish control. Her hands unclenched. The tight-ness in her chest lessened, and she was breathing more easily. "That's better."

"Are you ready to go back and face the media?"

"Why not? The worst that can happen is that I'll sell a few more cakes."

Grateful for his support, she reached toward him. With her thumb, she rubbed a smear of flour off his cheek. This time, she didn't say thanks. Didn't need to.

IT WAS almost noon when Cody escorted Rue into the downtown police station to view a lineup of suspects.

He'd canceled his schedule for the rest of the day, sending his overworked secretary into a state of panic. His firm was in the midst of year-end corporate investments and oil-lease negotiations. In these dealings, Cody had the opportunity to shine, to ensure that he'd be named partner next year.

But his career was less important than answering the question that had plagued him since he was a kid: who killed his father? Staying close to Rue gave him access to the police investigation.

At the police station, he sat beside her in the square plastic chairs against the walls of a bland beige corridor. He toyed with the idea of turning over the Danny Mason bumper sticker and the shamrock tiepin that had been delivered to him last week. Cody already knew there was no forensic evidence to be obtained from those objects. His private detective had already checked for fingerprints and trace evidence like hairs and bits of lint. There was nothing.

However, given the fact that the same gun killed Lindahl and his father, those objects might provide a clue.

Or not. After years of failed investigation, he lacked confidence in the Denver PD. They didn't even seem to be linking the two murders. The homicide detective in charge, Aaron Abbott, hadn't even spoken to him. If it weren't for Danny's phone call last night, Cody wouldn't have known about the murder weapon.

Rue leaned her shoulder against his and said, "I

can't believe they already have a lineup. When Detective Abbott stopped by the shop earlier with a photo array, I didn't recognize anybody."

"The police must have gotten an ID from the other two witnesses. Tyler Zubek and Carlos."

"I wonder if Carlos is out of the hospital."

She glanced over at the bodyguard who had driven them downtown. "Did you hear anything about the other witnesses? Or the suspects?"

"Nope."

Mel the bodyguard was a former cop. Though he was a big guy with heavy shoulders, a beer belly and almost no neck, he had an aura of watchful stillness and professionalism. Cody wondered if the bodyguard had left the police force by choice or if he'd been fired. "We could use more information, Mel. Do you have some friends down here you could talk to?"

"I never worked in Denver. I'm from Grand Junction."

"Why did you quit police work?"

"Personal security pays better."

If that were true, Mel hadn't been working for low-rent clients. He provided security for people with money—people Cody might know. But he didn't recall ever seeing Mel before. "Did you ever work for Bob Lindahl?"

"Sure did."

"Why do you think he got shot?"

Mel hitched his thumbs in his jeans' pockets and

looked down at the carpeted floor. "I don't talk about clients. Living or dead."

A solid ethical position. Cody couldn't fault the bodyguard for lack of discretion.

An unsmiling Detective Abbott approached them. "Ms. Harris, come with me."

Cody stood beside her. "I'll be accompanying Ms. Harris. I'm an attorney."

"I know who you are, Mr. Berringer."

He met the detective's gaze. "Then you know why I'm especially interested in this case."

"The murder weapon." Abbott gave a brisk nod. "I'll be frank with you, Mr. Berringer. Our investigation centers on the current crime."

Anger clenched his gut. How the hell could the police turn a blind eye to his father's murder? "Let me get this straight. You think the use of the same murder weapon in two crimes is a coincidence."

"That Colt .45 could have changed hands several times in the past twenty years."

"Lindahl and my father knew each other," Cody said through tight lips. "They were part of the same investigations. You can't ignore those connections."

"This is my investigation."

"And you're doing a piss-poor job of it." Getting mad wouldn't do any good, but there was nothing more infuriating than incompetence. "Lindahl's killer purposely left the gun behind. He was sending a message."

"Step back, Mr. Berringer." The detective looked toward Rue. "Ms. Harris, come with me."

"Actually," she said, "I'd like Mr. Berringer to be with me. He's my attorney."

A lie. Cody hadn't practiced criminal law in years, but he was grateful to Rue. She understood how important it was for him to be involved in this investigation.

Detective Abbott gave a curt nod. "Both of you. Let's go."

Rue picked up a white cardboard box printed on top with the logo for Ruth Ann's Cakes. "This is for you, Detective. And for the other officers in the break room. Cupcakes with milk-chocolate frosting."

Abbott was nonplussed. "What?"

"When I was a kid and came to the station with my stepfather, I must have swiped a couple of dozen donuts. This is payback. Take it."

He accepted the box. "Please, Ms. Harris. Will you come with me now?"

"I'd like my bodyguard to accompany us."

"Fine." Abbott was beaten; his gaze was weary. "Anybody else? Maybe some of the women who work at your cake shop?"

"Why would you say that?"

"Your cake shop has been all over the television news."

Defiantly, Rue stuck out her chin. "I didn't say anything the reporters didn't already know. Somebody else had already spoken to the media."

"You did okay," the detective conceded.

Finally, they started down the hallway. Rue spoke to the detective. "How did my shop look on the news?"

"Not bad," he said. "What's the name of that blond woman who runs your cash register?"

"Bernice Layne. She's single."

"Is she?"

Cody noticed the evil glint in Rue's eye as she listed the many fine attributes of blond Bernice, leaving out the important detail that Bernice was a cross-dresser.

Rue was so damned cute and feisty that Cody could have kissed her. Unlike most people, she wasn't intimidated by police procedure. It made sense that she wouldn't be nervous; she'd grown up around cops.

In a small room with a large window, they joined two other attorneys: one from the DA's office and one who was representing someone in the lineup. After the detective explained the procedure, six men entered the adjoining room in single file and stood facing them. Each man held a number.

"Take your time," the detective said. "Can you identify the man who shot Bob Lindahl?"

Her brow furrowed as she squinted and tilted her head to one side, then the other.

Cody made his own assessment. All of the six men were similar height and build. All appeared to be in their late thirties or early forties—old enough to have murdered his father twenty years ago. The mere hint that he might finally be face-to-face with his father's killer sent an electric shock down his spine. *Was it one of these men?*

Instead of studying their features, he looked for the tell-tale body language of guilt: a shifting gaze, a nervous twitch, a tension in the jaw or forehead. Two of the men in the lineup—number two and number three—had bad cases of the jitters. But if Cody had been picking out a cold-blooded assassin, he'd point to number five, whose dark eyes were cold and vacant.

Rue stepped back from the window. "I'm sorry, Detective. I can't tell."

"Take another look."

"The man who shot Bob Lindahl wore a sweat-shirt with the hood up and dark glasses. And there was something weird about his nose—almost as if it was fake." She shook her head. "I was concentrating more on his gun than his face."

One of the attorneys in the back of the room spoke up. "That's a negative ID. She can't pick my client out."

"But our other two witnesses were definite," said the attorney from the DA's office. "And your client has no alibi. He's under arrest for the murder of Robert Lindahl."

For the first time since they'd arrived at the police station, Rue appeared agitated. "Are you telling me that Carlos and Tyler recognized him? They identified him?"

"That's right."

Her hazel eyes darkened, and the corners of her mouth tightened. Cody was beginning to understand her expressions. Her frown signaled self-doubt. He knew she was blaming herself for not being as alert as the other witnesses.

"Which one?" Rue asked. "Which guy in the lineup?"

"I can't give you that information," the detective said. "Don't want to prejudice your testimony if this case comes to trial."

"Does this mean it's over? You've got the man who shot Bob Lindahl?"

Before answering, Detective Abbott shot a glance toward Cody. He seemed to be deciding how much he ought to reveal. When he spoke, he hedged, "We're about to arrest a suspect. That's all I can tell you."

Not much of an answer, and Cody had a lot more questions. Was there forensic evidence? What was the name and past history of the accused? More than anything else, he wanted to know where the accused got that gun.

Unfortunately, Detective Abbott wasn't compelled to tell them a damn thing. This was police business. Not their concern.

"I need to ask one thing," Cody said. It was the main question, the most important question. "Will Ms. Harris be safe?"

"I'm satisfied that we have the right man in custody," the detective said.

"Are you sure?" Rue asked. "I couldn't pick him out of the lineup, but maybe you've got other evidence. Like fingerprints or DNA or something. What about his vehicle? I got a good look at the car. Shouldn't I take a look and see if I can identify his car?"

He held up his hand like a traffic cop stopping the flow of her words. He took a step away from her and turned his back. Over his shoulder, he said, "Thanks for the cupcakes."

Chapter Seven

Rue spent the rest of the afternoon in the kitchen at her shop, preparing the four-tier tartan cake for tomorrow's wedding while Bernice and the weekend crew handled the walk-in customers.

Rue's van had been returned by the police. She'd been notified by the clean-up people that her house was back together. And a suspect in the murder of Bob Lindahl had been arrested. She should have been relieved.

But she wasn't.

The super-fast police investigation felt somehow anti-climactic. She worried because their case seemed to be based entirely on the testimony of the other two witnesses, and it was hard to believe they were more observant than she was.

She concentrated on the task at hand: the Scottish wedding cake. She'd frosted the top of each layer in creamy white chocolate. The sides were covered with smooth fondant that she was hand-painting in a red, white, blue and black tartan. The crisp, precise lines were making her cross-eyed.

She sat back on the stool and rested her hand on the countertop. How could Carlos and Tyler Zubek have positively identified the man in the hooded sweatshirt? He was wearing dark glasses. And she thought his nose was fake. They'd only had a glimpse of him. How could they be so sure?

Cody shared her doubts about their identification. After he'd dropped her off at the shop, he'd gone to his office to contact people who could give him information about the police investigation. There had to be something more, something the police weren't telling them.

If so, she was sure that Cody would find out. When it came to anything related to his father's murder, he was ferocious. His forehead tensed, and his voice took on a low, dangerous tone. He reminded her of the Golden Gloves boxers Danny used to know. Scary and intense.

Bernice flounced into the kitchen and stood beside her, staring at the cake. "It's fabulous."

"The tartan is going to look really great with the rest of the wedding decorations. Bouquets of wild-flowers and heather."

"Are the men wearing kilts?"

"You bet they are," Rue said. Her mother, the wedding planner, had outfitted the five groomsmen in full Scottish attire. "Plus the three bagpipers."

"I love a man in a skirt," Bernice said as she delivered a cup of black coffee to Mel who had positioned himself so he could see both the front of the shop and the rear entrance. "How about it, Mel? Ever wear a skirt?"

"Not in this lifetime."

"But you'd be so cute," she teased. "Just like me."

"Nobody's like you."

Though his voice was gruff, there was a twinkle in his eye. Throughout the day, Mel and Bernice had discovered that they had several things in common, including an interest in opera.

"By the way," Rue said to Bernice, "do you remember that homicide detective, Aaron Abbott?"

"Nice eyes. Bad haircut. He liked the cinnamon rolls."

"When we were down at the police station, he asked about you."

Her eyes brightened. Though Bernice was seldom lacking for boyfriends, she'd been going through a dry spell. "I wonder if Detective Abbott would wear a kilt."

Mel scoffed. "Doubtful."

Rue picked up her brush again. All that was left on this cake was the tartan on the top layer. "I ought to be done here in about an hour. Bernice, if you want to take off, go ahead."

"I believe I will, since I'm coming in early tomorrow."

Rue glanced toward Mel. "You could go, too. Since the police have made an arrest, I really don't need a bodyguard anymore."

"Danny hired me," Mel said. "He's the one who says when the job is over."

"Get him on your cell phone. I'll talk to him."

Returning her attention to the tartan icing, she carefully filled out the edges on a line of red. Was she being too hasty in dismissing her bodyguard? Detective Abbott was fairly sure that he had the right guy in custody, and he seemed like a decent cop. She wanted to believe she was safe.

When Mel held out his cell phone, she set down her paintbrush and took it. "Danny?"

"This is Jerome. Danny's in a meeting with the Denver trash collectors."

"Apparently, that takes precedence over the murder of his best friend and a threat to my life."

"Don't be a whiner." In his tone, she heard echoes of her childhood when she had resented Jerome for taking too much of Danny's time. And he had probably resented her for the same reason. "You're always bragging about how you can take care of yourself."

"I can," she said.

"Then shape up. In case you haven't noticed, Danny has other things to think about. He's the new mayor. Not that you had anything to do with the campaign."

"I did what you told me," she said coldly. "I stayed out of the picture while Danny posed with his new wife and stepchildren."

"A lot of good that did," he grumbled. "Now you're front and center on the evening news. You and Leticia."

"Sorry to inconvenience you by witnessing a murder."

Though he laughed, the sound was as tight as a creaky hinge. "Why did you call?"

"To thank Danny for the bodyguard and to tell him that I don't need protection anymore. The police took a suspect into custody."

"I heard. Fast work."

Maybe too fast. "Do you know anything else about their investigation? Like the name of the suspect?"

"Roy Madigan, aka Mad Dog Madigan. He has a rap sheet as long as your arm and did time for armed robbery."

"Any idea why he attacked Lindahl?"

"A grudge killing," Jerome said. "Lindahl was the first cop who arrested Madigan."

That must have been a very long time ago. Lindahl had left the force and gone into construction full time almost eighteen years ago.

She remembered that transition because Danny had been upset, even though they'd all known it was coming. Lindahl had been talking about his plans to be a big-time construction mogul for as long as she'd known him. The first present he'd given her was a beautiful slate-blue dollhouse with blue trim. Lindahl had made it himself, and the detail was incredible. Whatever had happened to that dollhouse? She hadn't seen it in years. Though her relationship with Lindahl was never as cozy as he'd thought, she wouldn't mind having the dollhouse as a remembrance.

"Rue?" She heard Jerome's voice over the phone. "Are you still there?"

"Just thinking," she said. "Didn't you work for Lindahl?"

"Summers on construction," he said. "Heavy work, but it helped me pay for college."

She heard a hint of pride and bitterness in his tone—a reminder of how hard Jerome had worked to overcome his difficult childhood. As if nobody else had ever had to struggle?

"Tell Danny thanks for the bodyguard," she said. "But I ought to be safe now."

"I'll tell him."

She handed the cell phone back to Mel. "You're officially relieved of your duties."

"It's been interesting, ladies." He finished off his coffee and handed the cup back to Bernice. "In case you need me again. I'll leave my card on your desk."

Bernice gave Rue a hug. "I'm going, too. And you have a good time tonight with your young man. He's a babe."

That he was. Cody was a definite babe. But a good time? Rue wasn't so sure.

CODY ARRIVED at Rue's shop later than he'd intended. It was already dark when he stepped inside. Though the lights were on and the gingerbread town in the front window hadn't been moved, the display shelves behind the counter were empty. The tabletops had been wiped, the tile floor washed. The place seemed deserted, but that couldn't be. Rue would never leave the front door unlocked.

An unreasonable panic gripped him. What if she'd been attacked? What if she was lying on the kitchen floor in a pool of blood?

When she appeared in the doorway leading from the kitchen, he felt like scooping her into his arms and kissing her sweet face. "Where were you?" he demanded.

"Admiring my own handiwork," she admitted. "Come back here and take a look."

"Why are you here alone? Where's Mel?"

"I sent him home. The police caught the killer so I'm safe. Don't need a bodyguard." She waved her hands, motioning him toward her. "Get yourself over here and see what a genius I am."

He followed her into the kitchen which had also been scrubbed clean. The overhead light gleamed on the countertops and appliances. She opened the door to a walk-in refrigeration unit. "Voila!"

Inside were shelves packed with neatly labeled ingredients and completed bakery products. Standing on a metal cart in the center of the unit was a four-tier cake with tartan-trimmed sides and fancy white icing flourishes decorated with real flowers.

He'd watched her at work and knew she could bake, but this cake was more like art—a sculpture with icing. Until now, he hadn't appreciated her skill. "How did you get that plaid on the sides?"

"Hand-painted." She was obviously pleased with herself. Smiling and sunny. "It took forever."

"Impressive. You've got talent."

"You bet I do." She closed the door to the refrigeration unit. "How about you? What did you accomplish this afternoon?"

"The suspect's name is Madigan. Has a criminal record. Did six years for armed robbery. Bob Lindahl was the cop who arrested him the first time, and the police assume the murder was payback."

She took off her apron and headed toward the office on the opposite side of the kitchen. "Did you find any connection with your father's murder?"

"No." Cody had researched court records from twenty years ago. When his father was with the district attorney's office, he hadn't prosecuted Mad Dog Madigan. The first arrest—the one made by Lindahl—happened a year after his father was dead. "There was no indication that my father and Madigan ever met."

"Disappointed?"

"I'm mad as hell."

"Why?"

"The murder weapon should be enough to get the police to reopen their investigation into my father's killing, but they're ignoring that angle."

They'd brushed off his inquiries with vague talk of coincidence and statistics about how many times a weapon could change hands over the years. Cody knew better. The solution to his father's murder was tied to Lindahl's killing, and he intended to figure it out…with or without official police sanction.

"Is there any other evidence on Madigan?" Rue asked. "Anything more than the witness identification?"

"A footprint."

"How could they tell it belonged to the killer? There were nearly a hundred people coming in and out of the house."

"My thought exactly."

She unfastened her ponytail and shook her head. Her long chestnut hair cascaded over her slender shoulders. Even after a full day that had started before dawn, her appearance was fresh and wholesome, her cheeks rosy, her skin glistening. Rue was beginning to grow on him. The more he was around her, the prettier she became.

"You know," she said, "I'd feel a lot better if the police had more convincing proof."

"Here's something." He set his attaché on the desk in her office and flipped it open. "This is a photograph of Madigan's car. Do you recognize it?"

She held the picture in her hand and stared, then slowly shook her head. "This wasn't the car I shot at. Why didn't Detective Abbott show me this picture?"

"The vehicle can't be considered identification. It could belong to somebody else. Could be stolen."

"But you don't believe that."

"I don't," he admitted. "The official case against Madigan stands on two shaky legs. A vague motive.

And two witnesses who picked him out of a lineup. I think the police have the wrong guy."

"Madigan's not the killer?"

Her greenish-gray eyes searched his face, looking for the truth. "I wish I could give you the easy answer, Rue. But I think the killer is still out there. You should get your bodyguard back."

Her lips pursed as she considered. "I've been thinking about this. Weighing the options. Deciding what to do."

"About what?"

"If the police made a mistake, I'm the one who could get hurt. The killer could come after me. Again. He already trashed my home. I don't want to sit around and wait for another break-in."

He nodded. "Which is why you call Mel."

"I think we should investigate. You and me. On our own."

From the first moment he'd met Rue, he'd wanted to use her contacts. She had the inside track with Danny. Being with her opened doors for him.

But his feelings for her had changed. He cared about her. He sure as hell didn't want to see her hurt. "It's not safe for you to be involved."

"It's more dangerous if the killer is still out there, still wanting revenge against me." She tossed her apron into a hamper and slipped on her suede jacket. "And I know exactly where to start. We need to have a little chat with Tyler Zubek. To find out why he identified Madigan in the lineup."

Her plan didn't sound too radical. "Do you know how to reach him?"

"We went to high school together. If Tyler isn't listed in the phone book, I can talk to his mother."

"The direct approach." If Cody marched up to the doorstep of Tyler Zubek's mother, he'd face resistance. People didn't like talking to lawyers. "What makes you think his mother will help you?"

"Because I'm a nice girl. And I come bearing cake."

Chapter Eight

Rue's plan to locate Tyler Zubek turned out to be more complicated than a quick phone call. Mrs. Zubek didn't actually remember Rue from high school, but she'd seen Ruth Ann's Cakes on the news and fallen in love with the gingerbread town. Rue promised her a free cake, and Mrs. Zubek responded with three surefire ways to contact her son.

However, when Rue called Tyler's cell, it went directly to voice mail. His girlfriend was another dead end. Her third contact was a project supervisor at Lindahl Construction who told her that Tyler might be hanging drywall at a new housing development called Prairie Haven. According to his boss, they were behind schedule, and Tyler often stayed late.

Following directions from the project supervisor, she and Cody headed northeast toward the airport. Five and a half miles off the highway, they found Prairie Haven—a large construction project of more than eighty single-family homes. Formerly, this land had been fallow—rolling hills covered by weeds and buffalo grass. If there had ever been trees on this windswept terrain, they were leveled when Lindahl Construction put in water and electricity.

On the brand-new roads, she peered through the windshield at houses in varying stages of construction. Though streetlights shone brightly in the still night, the lack of landscaping and the silence created an air of emptiness.

"Prairie Haven is a little creepy," she said. "Nothing is supposed to live out here but prairie dogs, rattlesnakes and coyotes."

"Within twenty years this area will be covered with houses," he predicted.

Like all true Colorado natives, she was wary of too much sprawl, too much stress on the natural environment, too many people breathing the mountain air. "Do you really think Denver will get that big?"

"If they figure out a way to develop the oil shale on the western slope, bigger."

"Is that good for your business?" she asked.

He nodded. "A lot of my clients are oil companies, and I'm in favor of growth. I don't buy the romanticized view that Denver is a sleepy little cow town."

In his cashmere overcoat and monogrammed shirts, he looked like a big-city guy. "You're not a romantic. That's for sure."

"I do okay in the romance department."

"You've never been married," she said.

"Neither have you."

"At least I'm open to the possibility." Rue wasn't anxious to get married, but she had already planned her wedding cake. "Are you? Open to it?"

"I don't think about it."

And she knew why. His bitterness about the unresolved murder of his father didn't leave room for other commitments. He didn't really care about anything else. Or anyone else.

In the reflected light from the dashboard and the streetlamps, she studied him, trying to see past his perfect black hair, blue eyes and chiseled profile. Who was the man inside that handsome exterior? She'd caught glimpses when he'd rushed to protect her and when he'd worked in the kitchen at her shop. And when she'd kissed him.

Remembering how good she'd felt in his arms, she exhaled a wistful sigh. No use in thinking about kisses and the possibility of a relationship. Not with a man who was obsessed with a twenty-year-old murder. Not with Cody.

Rue pulled her attention back to the deserted streets. "With all these backhoes and building supplies, I'm surprised there isn't a night watchman."

"I'm sure there is," he said. "We just haven't run into him yet."

"How will we know where to find Tyler?"

"He's hanging drywall, so he has to be working in one of the nearly completed houses. The electricity would have to be hooked up. Look for lights coming from inside the house."

They rounded a corner into a cul-de-sac where three houses were lit up. There was a pickup parked at the curb. Tyler's vehicle?

Cody pulled up behind it. "Let's start here."

A shiver of apprehension went down her spine; she didn't want to leave the safety of Cody's Mercedes. Her nervousness deepened as he reached into the glove compartment and took out the gun he'd brandished at her shop this morning.

"Is that necessary?"

"I hope not."

She stepped out of the car into the stillness of the chilly December night. In the distance, she saw the glittering lights of Denver.

Shivering inside her suede jacket, she pulled on her mittens and glanced at the half circle of empty houses. "Who do you think will take over Lindahl Construction?"

"I looked into that," he said. "Though I don't know the contents of his will, I assume that his sister will get a big slice of the pie. I doubt his ex-wives will benefit financially from his death. And he had no kids."

"I know."

With his gun tucked inside the pocket of his overcoat, Cody started up the winding sidewalk to the front door of a midsized split-level house on a dusty lot. "Lindahl was mortgaged to the hilt. The bulk of his estate will be divvied up among his investors. It's a long list."

"Any name pop out?"

"Danny."

Once again, Danny figured into the picture. Biting back her automatic defense of her former stepfather, she asked, "Do you think any of these investors—like Danny—would kill Lindahl to get their money back?"

"Not a viable motive," he said. "If an investor wanted their cash, they'd have taken Lindahl to court. He had assets."

They were at the front door. Cody twisted the knob and pushed it open. "Hello," he called out. "Anybody here?"

His voice echoed. With no furniture, no appliances and most of the finishing work not done, the house was a skeleton without a heart. "Tyler Zubek?" she said loudly. "Tyler, are you in here?"

Cody strode from the entryway into the living room and quickly explored the main level. The heels of his polished wingtips echoed on the bare floor boards. "It's empty. Let's go next door."

They returned to the street. There were no tree branches to rattle in the light breeze, but the wind had its own song. A low moan.

When Cody cut across the dirt toward the next house, she ran to keep up. "Like I said before. It's creepy out here."

"There's something weird about this," he agreed. "Why would Tyler be here alone? Drywalling goes a lot faster with a crew."

"Maybe he needed the overtime. His mother

thought that he and his girlfriend were getting serious. Tyler could be saving up for a wedding." She searched her mind for other plausible explanations. "Maybe he just needed some time alone."

Cody glanced over his shoulder. "Could be that he needed a place where he could meet someone else and be sure there were no witnesses."

"Why?"

When they stood on the doorstep of the second house, he looked down at her. "You're not going to like my theory."

"Why not?"

"Because you like to think the best of people, and it's possible that Tyler wasn't behaving in an entirely ethical manner."

She had no personal investment in Tyler Zubek. They'd gone to the same high school but weren't friends. "What's your theory?"

"Tyler fingered Madigan. He might have been paid to make that identification."

"A conspiracy?"

"Nothing that complicated," he said. "Just a pay-off to make sure Tyler picked Madigan out of the lineup. He could have arranged a meeting here to get his money."

"You think he was dealing with the murderer?"

"It's possible."

Cody shoved open the door to the second house, and they entered.

Again, the lights were on, but nobody was home.

She was beginning to think that she didn't want to find Tyler Zubek. Would he take a payoff to identify the wrong man? But Carlos had made the same identification. Were they both lying?

"Over here," Cody called to her.

She followed his voice to the lower level, an area that would probably be a family room. Sheets of drywall were stacked against a wall. Cody hunkered down beside a metal toolbox and a nail gun. "This must have been where Tyler was working."

"Do you think we missed him?"

"He wouldn't leave his toolbox." Cody stood. "And we saw a pickup parked in front. He's not far from here."

A sense of foreboding tightened her throat. She swallowed hard and said, "Let's leave. We can find Tyler tomorrow."

"There's only one more lighted house. We might as well check it out."

As she stepped outside, she sensed a difference in the atmosphere. A tension that hadn't been there before. The December chill bit her cheeks. Peering down the street, she saw another vehicle parked near the corner. "Cody, look."

He was already halfway across the dirt yard. Turning, he asked, "What is it?"

She pointed toward the car. That dark sedan could have been the same car she'd seen at Lindahl's house. "Somebody else is here."

And she was standing on a lighted porch like a big,

fat target. Her survival instinct kicked in, and she darted down the steps to the sidewalk.

Three gunshots exploded in the night.

Racing toward her, Cody grabbed her arm and pulled her around the corner of the house. Side by side, breathing hard, they flattened themselves against the wall.

He reached into his pocket and pulled out his cell phone. "Call 911," he said. "I'm going to return fire. He needs to know that I'm armed."

She tore off her mittens to punch the buttons on the phone. It rang. And rang.

Cody stepped out from shelter, fired once and returned to her side. "We've got to move. He knows where we are."

Still holding the phone, she followed him to the back of the house. Finally, the 911 operator answered.

"We're being shot at," Rue said into the phone. "We're at Prairie Haven development, northeast of Denver."

After a pause, the operator said, "Can you give me more information about your location?"

This area wouldn't be on any maps. "Northeast. It's off Big Horn Road. Nobody lives here yet. It's still being built. Lindahl Construction."

At the rear of the house, Cody signaled for her to stop. Carefully, he peered around the corner into the backyard. The light from the house windows slanted across the dirt.

The operator asked, "Could I have your name?"

"Rue Harris. Ruth Ann."

"The woman with the cake shop? I saw you on the news."

"Great." Now wasn't the time to exchange recipes. "Somebody is shooting at us."

"Stay on the line, please. I'll check your location."

Cody turned to her. "We need to move. Otherwise, he'll know exactly where we are."

"Move? Where?"

"Run to the house next door." He gestured with the gun. "I'll cover you. Go."

She took off, running as fast as she could across the uneven soil. Her ankle jolted, but she kept going. Later, she would feel the pain.

There were no lights in this house. The only illumination came from the half-moon and stars overhead.

Cody raced up beside her. Barely pausing, he indicated their next move. "Across the yard."

If there had been people living here, the yard would have been grass and there would be fences. She stared across an open stretch of dirt clods. Though the distance could be measured in feet, it seemed like miles. "There's no cover."

"I'll stay close to you."

The 911 operator was saying something, but Rue didn't listen. She ducked low to minimize herself as a target and started running. Cody was beside her. His black overcoat flapped like the wings of a hawk.

She heard another gunshot. Cody fired back.

They were at a dark house on a different street from

where their car was parked. He directed her toward the front, then to another house and another. Her heart pounded. She was sweating in spite of the cold. Somewhere in their escape, she'd lost one of her mittens.

They dodged from one house to another. When they finally stopped running, she had no idea where they were. Gasping, she asked, "How will we get back to the car?"

"It's in front of the only three houses with lights on."

"And if he turns the lights off?"

"We're in trouble." He pulled her close. "Don't worry. I'll get you out of this."

She wanted to believe him. He seemed to have a plan. But a man with a gun was after them, and she had every reason to believe their pursuer was a professional killer who had already outsmarted the police once.

For a few brief seconds, she nested in Cody's warmth. He was a big man—strong and capable. He'd rescued her before. She wanted to believe he could do it again.

"There he is," he whispered.

She pulled away from him and stared across the dirt landscape. Their pursuer was a shadow, a dark figure in a hooded sweatshirt.

As she watched, he disappeared behind the house across from them.

Lifting the cell phone to her ear, she whispered, "Are you there?"

The operator answered, "Stay calm, Ruth Ann."

Not much chance of that. "Have you found our location? Prairie Haven development. Big Horn Road."

"We'll find you. Stay on the line."

She hadn't answered Rue's question.

Cody sighted down the barrel of his gun. Aiming carefully.

"Don't." She touched his arm. "If you shoot, he'll know where we are."

He lowered the weapon. "You're right. I don't think I can be accurate at this distance."

"We can't keep running like rats in a maze."

"Maybe we can set a trap."

"That's good. Rats in a maze setting a mouse trap."

"A joke?" He grinned. "You're cool enough to make jokes?"

"I plan to collapse in terror later." She shuddered. "What kind of trap?"

"I'll start running, make a lot of noise. I'll draw his attention."

"What about me?"

"Run like hell to the car."

"By myself?" She hated his plan. When she was with Cody, she felt safer. At least there were two of them. "Danny used to tell me that you never went anywhere without backup. I don't want to split up."

"And I don't want to wait for him to find us. It's only a matter of time, Rue."

"You might be right," she conceded. In these silent streets, their pursuer would probably locate them no matter how many times they doubled back.

He placed his car keys in her hand. "Get my car, drive back here and pick me up."

"I don't know where we are." Her voice quavered. "These streets aren't marked."

"Which is why it's taking the cops so damn long to respond. We can't keep dashing from place to place. Too random. We could run right into him."

Under her breath, she let out a stream of curses she seldom used. "Okay, I'll do it."

He pointed. "You go that way. Look for the houses with lights. I'll take the opposite direction."

She looked up into his blue eyes, aware that his might be the last face she ever saw. This wasn't a game of cops and robbers. The man in the hooded sweatshirt played for keeps. Bob Lindahl was dead. As she remembered the horrible crimson bloodstains on his holiday clothes, panic rushed through her. "I don't want to die."

Cody kissed her hard. She clung to him. Didn't want to leave his side. Wanted to be with him.

He peered deeply into her eyes. "You can do this."

"Okay, I'm ready."

"Now."

She darted to the left, passed a house that was still in the early stages of construction. Her gaze searched frantically. Where were the lights? Where were the houses they'd entered earlier? She dashed across the dirt yards to another house.

Behind her, she heard an exchange of gunfire. Cody! She stopped dead in her tracks. He could be hurt, killed like his father by an anonymous murderer. No! Fate couldn't be so cruel.

When she turned back around, she was even more disoriented. Though the houses were different, they all looked alike. Stumbling, she rounded one corner, then another. She couldn't tell which way she'd gone. Which way she'd been. Where the hell were the police?

Then she spotted the light from a window. There! Closer than she'd expected.

Running, she went toward the lighted house. Her feet hit pavement on the cul-de-sac. Almost there. She saw Cody's Mercedes. And the truck. And the dark sedan driven by the killer.

More gunshots. They seemed closer. She glanced back over her shoulder, terrified that she'd see the man in the hooded sweatshirt.

She held Cody's car keys out straight in front of her, ready to push the button that automatically unlocked the doors.

Her toe caught on the curb, and she sprawled face-down on the pavement. The impact knocked the breath out of her. She gasped. Her lungs ached, but she managed to stand. So close. His Mercedes was only a few yards away.

She forced herself to breathe. Shook her head to clear her vision…and realized that she'd dropped the car keys and the cell phone.

Her frantic gaze searched the ground. She dropped to her knees, trying to see behind clods of dirt.

The next gunshot was very close.

She had to find cover. Someplace to hide.

Lurching forward, she approached Cody's car. Locked, of course.

She went toward the pickup truck. A beat-up old thing. If she was in luck, Tyler hadn't locked it. Maybe he'd even left the keys in the ignition.

As if her luck would suddenly change? As if she'd finally catch a break?

Her fingers closed on the door handle and she yanked. It swung open.

She hauled herself inside. Slumped on the bench seat was the lifeless body of Tyler Zubek. He'd been shot in the head.

Chapter Nine

Cody heard the approach of police sirens. Finally.

He had tried to count his shots but lost track. He had one bullet left—or two. A difference that could mean life or death.

His plan to split up hadn't fooled the guy in the hooded sweatshirt. Instead of being drawn to go after Cody, he'd spotted Rue and took off after her. She was the focus, the target.

Cody's fault. He'd put her in mortal danger.

Now he was the pursuer, chasing after an armed man whom he only glimpsed between shadows.

On the street outside the lighted houses, Cody had seen Rue yank on the door to his car. Something had been wrong. She'd run to the pickup truck and gotten inside.

The guy in the sweatshirt ran toward the truck.

Barely taking aim, Cody fired.

His shot was enough to distract the son of a bitch. Instead of going after Rue, he swerved across the street, running toward his vehicle.

Though Cody couldn't see the license plates from this angle, he identified the make. A Chevy. Ten or eleven years old. Dark blue. Was that the car? The same car Rue had seen at Lindahl's?

The police sirens were louder. They had to be inside the development, weaving up and down the unmarked streets.

Cody concentrated on the man who had been chasing them. The illumination from the street light made him clearly visible. Raising his weapon, Cody squinted down the barrel and squeezed the trigger.

Click. Nothing. He was out of ammo.

The man in the sweatshirt entered his car. Without turning on the headlights, he sped away.

Cody ran across the sidewalk toward the truck, praying that Rue was safe inside, that she hadn't been hurt by his bad planning, his mistake. She'd wanted to stay together, and he should have listened to her. Should have trusted her instincts and the lessons she'd learned as a kid with Danny.

He opened the door to the pickup. Rue had wedged herself into the small space between the bench seat and the dashboard on the passenger side. Her head was down. Her hands covered her face.

Crumpled on the seat of the pickup was the lifeless body of Tyler Zubek. He looked like he'd been shot while sitting behind the steering wheel and had slumped to the right. The side of his head was a bloody mess but his face was untouched. His blank eyes stared in dull surprise.

When Cody touched Rue's arm, she flinched.

"You're safe," he said. "The shooter is gone."

And the police sirens were right on top of them. Blue and red lights flashed jagged patterns across the empty streets.

Keeping her head down, Rue untangled herself from her hiding place. When she placed her small hand in his, her flesh was ice-cold.

His heart wrenched. He hadn't meant for this to happen. Hadn't meant for her to endure another trauma. Coming out here to question Tyler hadn't seemed dangerous, but he should have known better. He shouldn't have put her at risk.

When he pulled her out of the truck and into his arms, she felt small and vulnerable as a robin with a broken wing. "I'm sorry, Rue. I'm so goddamned sorry."

She lifted her face. Her lips trembled. "I thought you didn't believe in apologies."

"I don't."

"Change of heart?"

"Yes." His heart filled with a tenderness he couldn't explain. She was precious to him; her safety mattered more than his own. "Are you all right?"

"I don't have a bullet in me. I tripped and fell when I was running to your car. Dropped the keys and couldn't find them."

"So you ran to the truck."

"And found Tyler." She exhaled a ragged breath.

Uniformed police approached with guns drawn.

One of them barked commands. "Step away from the truck. Put the gun down."

Cody dropped his gun and raised his hands. There was no point in arguing. No point in trying to explain that they should have been chasing a blue Chevy that was probably on its way to the highway.

Law enforcement had procedures they had to follow even when their rules and restrictions ran counter to logic and intelligence. He couldn't help thinking that if the cops had listened to him in the first place, none of this would have happened.

RUE PUT HER anxiety on hold while the police checked their identification and contacted the homicide detectives in charge of investigating the Lindahl murders. After they were cleared, she needed no convincing to go home with Cody that night. The instant he offered, she accepted. She didn't want to be alone.

Finding Tyler's body had been more difficult than seeing Lindahl shot down before her eyes. Tyler's death seemed unreal. He was her age. They'd gone to high school together. He was much too young to be dead. Murdered.

She crossed the plush carpet in Cody's condo, not stopping at the kitchen. The mere thought of food turned her stomach. All she wanted right now was a long, hot shower. The night chill had penetrated her bones, and she needed to thaw.

"I'm going to clean up," she said as she walked

toward the bathroom across the hall from the guest bedroom where she'd slept last night. Inside, she closed the door and leaned against it.

She was cold. And angry. And hurt. Her ankle was sore. Her palms were scraped from when she'd tripped and fallen on the pavement. Small injuries compared to what might have happened; she could have been killed.

What would have happened if she'd gone directly home from the shop? Would the killer have been there, waiting? He might have come later. Broken in after midnight. Shot her while she slept.

Her hand covered her mouth, holding back a sob. It was sheer luck that Cody had come back to the shop for her. He'd rescued her. Again.

She barely knew him, but he'd stood by her. Right now, it seemed as though he was the only person she could count on. Danny was too busy being mayor, and the police had made a big mistake, taking the wrong man into custody.

As she peeled off her clothes, she noticed blood-stains on her shirt and slacks. Tyler's blood.

Piling her hair on top of her head, she turned on the shower and stepped under the hot stream of water. Clouds of steam billowed around her.

When she closed her eyelids and turned her face up to the water, she saw Tyler's face. His sightless eyes. The smear of blood that traced the line of his cheek. He was only in his twenties. Like her.

She told herself not to think about it. *Push the*

memory away. Forget about it. Think about some-thing else.

Ever since she was a little girl, that had been the way she dealt with bad things. She closed her eyes and wished them into oblivion.

But she wasn't a child anymore. There would be no hiding from this reality; she had to deal with the danger. Somehow make sense of it. Who had killed Tyler Zubek?

Under the steady spray of the shower, her skin turned pink. It had been a very long day; she should have been exhausted and ready for sleep. But her nerves were coiled tightly. She needed to figure this out, needed to talk to Cody.

Out of the shower, she glared at her bloodstained clothing. No way could she ever wear that outfit again. Wrapped in a white terrycloth robe that hung on the door of the guest-room shower, she padded into the front room.

In the sunken living room with the spectacular view of night sky and city lights through the win-dows, Cody was waiting. He'd prepared a drink for her. And a plate of cheese and crackers.

She went for the vodka and orange juice and took a long sip. She was ready to deal with the situation.

"Here's the thing," she said. "If Tyler was bribed to identify Madigan and went to Prairie Haven to get his payoff, why was he killed?"

"Second thoughts," Cody said. "Maybe Tyler

came to his senses and changed his mind about lying to the police."

"Why would he tell the bad guy?" She combed her fingers through her damp hair, spreading it across her shoulders to dry. "Tyler wasn't the sharpest knife in the drawer, but he wouldn't have gone alone and unarmed to face a cold-blooded killer. Especially not if he meant to back out of their deal."

"True." He stared into his own drink as if expecting an answer to emerge. "Tyler might have intended to ask for more money."

"Extortion? Of a cold-blooded killer?"

"Greed makes people do stupid things," he said. "The trick to blackmail is knowing how much money you can ask for without getting caught."

"Really? And how do you know about blackmail?"

"It's not all that different from any other business negotiation. Tyler could provide a service for the killer by throwing the police off the scent. After the first taste of cash, he decided his so-called service was worth a bigger payoff. But he was wrong. Fatally wrong."

Lounging on his chocolate-brown sofa with his shirtsleeves rolled up to the elbows, Cody seemed absolutely relaxed and untroubled. He looked at her over the rim of his glass. His blue eyes shimmered.

She sat on the sofa adjacent to the one where he was sitting and adjusted the folds of the bathrobe, acutely aware of the fact that she was naked underneath. "Do you think he knew the killer?"

"It's possible." He frowned into his glass. "We'll never know for sure."

"Unless Tyler told someone else. Like his girlfriend. We should talk to her."

"Not our job," he said. "The police will interrogate the girlfriend and Tyler's other close associates. This time, maybe, they won't screw it up."

"I don't want to take that chance. I want to keep investigating on our own."

"Not a good idea."

"But the police have it all wrong. They're ignoring the obvious. This murder and Lindahl's murder are both tied to your father's death."

He set his drink on the glass-topped coffee table and sat beside her. His warm, intense focus made her feel like the only woman in the world. "I'm glad that you believe in me, Rue."

"This isn't about you. It's logical."

Though she clung to that thread of rational thinking, her common sense was fading fast. She wanted to kiss him, to melt into his arms, to feel his hands on her body.

"I learned something tonight." He rested his arm on the back of the sofa and leaned closer. "When you were in danger, I was scared. More scared than I've ever been in my life. If anything had happened to you…" He shook his head as if to erase that thought. "Investigating on our own will put you in more danger. It's better if you step aside."

"And wait for the killer to come after me?" She

took another taste of her vodka and set the glass beside his on the coffee table. "The police don't have the manpower to guard me 24/7. And I can't go into hiding."

"Why not? If you wanted to take a vacation in the mountains, I'd pay for it. There's a nice little place in Breckenridge."

"I have a business to run." And her business was taking off, partly due to the attention from the murder. Though she ought to feel guilty about capitalizing on tragedy, she hadn't asked to be thrust into the spotlight. As Bernice always said, any publicity was good.

When she leaned back on the sofa, he touched her shoulder. His fingers curled the ends of her hair. "I care about you. Need to be careful with you. To protect you like a delicate porcelain sculpture."

"I'm tough," she said. "Porcelain is also used to make the kitchen sink."

He grinned. "Okay, tough girl. How about a back rub?"

She should have pushed him away. They barely knew each other, and she still didn't completely trust his motives. Back rubs had a way of leading to more intimacy. She shouldn't…

But his fingers on the back of her neck felt much too wonderful. More. She wanted more.

Before she realized what she was doing, Rue had stretched out on his sofa on her belly, offering her back like a cat waiting to be petted.

He stroked gently at first, then deeper. His fingers

skillfully kneaded her shoulders and neck. Her tension released in little crackles and snaps, and she abandoned herself to sheer pleasure. She moaned. "Feels good."

"It's good for me, too," he murmured. "Your skin is like satin."

Cody loosened her robe and slid the sleeves down, displaying more of her soft, feminine body. He couldn't help but notice that she wasn't wearing a bra. Or anything else.

He massaged the tension points near her nape, and she moaned again—a sexy purr of contentment that buzzed in his ears and aroused his body. He might have faked his initial attraction to Rue, but there was nothing phony about his response to her now. He was hot and hard as a rock.

"Lower," she said. "Below my shoulder blades."

"Your robe is in the way."

She wriggled on the sofa, freeing her arms from the sleeves and raising them above her head. "Lower," she repeated. "Now."

His gaze feasted on her petal-soft skin. The line of her spine. The curve of her tiny waist. She was all woman. Soft and pliant.

His hands tingled as he stroked her back. He leaned against her, pressing his erection against her thigh. He wanted to make love to her, to bury himself in her sweet, soft body. But he wouldn't take advantage of her or give her false expectations. It was best to come clean and tell the truth.

"The first time I saw you…" His voice was husky with desire and lust. He cleared his throat. "When I first met you—"

"And you were wearing that goofy Santa suit."

"Right," he said. "I asked you out because I wanted to get close to Danny. I was using you."

"I know," she said calmly. "Could you rub a little lower? At the base of my spine?"

"You knew?"

"You're a corporate shark with a rep for being a ladies' man. Not exactly the kind of guy who goes for a cake-baker."

"And you're okay with that?"

"Sure." She purred again. "I was using you, too. I wanted to sell you a wedding cake for your sister."

She was a hell of a lot more sophisticated than he gave her credit for. "Not exactly a naive little baker, are you?"

"Social climbing. Networking. Those were lessons learned at my mother's knee."

He should have guessed that the daughter of Leticia Wyndemere would know all about using people to get what you want. His question now was: What did Rue want?

Though he was aching to make love to her, he didn't want to disappoint her if she was looking for a commitment.

"If I picked you up and carried you into my bedroom, what would you expect?"

"I'm not sure what you're asking."

"Expectations," he said. "If I made love to you, would it mean…"

"That we're going steady?"

Laughing, she rolled onto her back. Her long, shining hair draped across her face. Her forearm shielded her breasts. Gazing up at him, she smiled, "If you make love to me, I expect that we'll have a real good time."

"And what else?"

"That's enough for me."

He leaned down and kissed that sultry little grin off her lips. She tasted like sex. The inside of her mouth was hot and slick.

Embracing her, he pulled her into a sitting position on the sofa. She wrestled herself around until she was on her knees. Her robe clung loosely to her hips as she pressed hard against him. Her breasts crushed against his chest.

There was nothing innocent about the way she maneuvered, the way she rubbed against his erection. Her aggression excited him. When he looked into her hazel eyes, he saw fire.

"You're full of surprises," he said.

"Meaning what?" Her breasts rose and fell with her heavy breathing.

"I thought you were a shy little wallflower."

"I'm not real good in groups." She ducked her head and nipped his earlobe. "One on one, I do okay."

"Better than okay."

Any guilt he might have felt vanished. This was a

woman who didn't play games. She told the truth and wasn't hesitant about making her desires known. He wanted to be the man who would fulfill her every wish, her every need.

"Well, Cody? Are you taking me to your bed or not?"

He scooped her off the sofa and carried her down the hall to his bedroom, dropping her on top of the comforter and diving down beside her.

She laughed and teased. She playfully helped as he tore off his clothes. They rolled across the king-size bed. First, he was on top. Then it was her turn.

Making love had never been this much fun. Guilt-free. Like her "Ruth-less" cakes.

Sheathed in a condom, he entered her with a hard thrust. She gasped and arched, drawing him into her again. He watched her eyes as she climaxed. The color changed from gray to green to a deep, dark gold. She was amazing.

He wanted to stay in bed with her forever. Because he didn't have to. They had made no commitment, no promises.

With Rue, he could have his cake and eat it, too.

Chapter Ten

The next day in the late afternoon, Cody stood beside Rue at the back of St. Jude's Episcopal Church. The "Wedding March" was being played by three bagpipers, so loudly that the stained glass shuddered in the five arched window frames on either side of the pews.

He shifted nervously as he watched the bride in her lacy white gown sail down the flower-draped aisle toward her groom who was wearing a kilt. Poor guy. He looked as if his toothpick legs were about to collapse.

Marriage was a deal that Cody would never make. Let other men get suckered into this primitive ritual with friends and family standing guard to make sure the vows would be fulfilled. As far as he was concerned, "I do" really meant "I won't." He'd heard the rules plenty of times. *I won't*…ever look at another woman. *I won't*…be bored with eating meatloaf at home every night. *I won't*…resent the intrusion on my time, being constantly monitored.

Not for him. He glanced down at Rue. Last night, their lovemaking had been phenomenal—even more so because there was no obligation or expectation.

They'd come to the Scottish wedding for two reasons. The first was business. Rue wanted to put in an appearance here and at the reception so people would remember who had baked the wedding cake. The second involved their investigation. The father of the bride was a police chief, which meant that several of the people here—including Danny—had been at Lindahl's house on the day of the murder.

At the front of the church, the minister began to recite the ceremony. Cody had seen enough. "Do we have to watch?"

She shook her head and tiptoed toward a side door that led away from the sanctuary. In a moment, they were outside the church, standing in a courtyard with a stone fountain in the center and statues of saints tucked into small niches around the edges.

The weather had turned cooler, more typical of December. Snow was predicted, and Cody was looking forward to spending tomorrow at home in his condo with Rue in his bed.

She looked cute today. After dropping off the tartan wedding cake at the downtown hotel where the reception would be held, they'd stopped at her duplex where she'd changed into a classic gray pant suit with pinstripes and a soft pink blouse that matched the bloom in her cheeks. Her long brown hair was twisted up on her head. A few wisps escaped and curled delicately on her nape.

He leaned down to inhale the vanilla scent that emanated from her and planted a little kiss below her ear.

She turned her head quickly, and he found himself kissing her lips. It was a very pleasant place to be.

Mel the bodyguard stalked toward them. Though Rue had dismissed him last night, Mel was reinstated after Tyler's murder. He grumbled under his breath, "Give it a rest. Can't you two keep your hands off each other?"

"Why should we?" Rue asked. Her eyes were wide and deceptively innocent. "Weddings are supposed to be romantic."

Cody didn't like that word. Romance wasn't on his agenda. He reminded himself that they had a solid investigative reason for being there.

Leticia—here in her role as wedding planner—stepped out of the church and joined them. Like Rue, Leticia wore a tailored suit. She glared up at the skies that had already begun to fade into sunset. "I hope the snow holds off until tomorrow. It'd be a shame for all these people to be forced to deal with bad weather on their ride home tonight."

"The wedding is going very well," Rue assured her mother. "The flowers in the church look wonderful."

"Have you delivered the cake?"

She gave a quick nod. "The ballroom at the hotel looks great, too."

"Too much tartan for my taste, but it was what they wanted. And the haggis." She shuddered. "That traditional Scottish dish is enough to turn me vegetarian."

"I like haggis," Mel said.

"You would." Leticia gave him a look that said bodyguards should be seen and not heard, then turned to Cody. "After what happened last night, I think it best for you and Rue not to attend the reception."

"Understood," Cody said. "You don't want bullets flying across the hors d'oeuvres."

"Certainly not." Almost as an afterthought, she added, "And I want my daughter to be safe."

"Thanks, Mom," Rue said politely. "I wanted to ask you about something. Do you remember a dollhouse that Bob Lindahl made for me? It was blue with white trim."

"Oh, yes. Very elaborate," Leticia said. "I remember Bob saying that it was the first house he ever built from the ground up. A Christmas present."

"I don't think it was for Christmas."

"Of course it was. I have a photo. I'll show you."

"Do you know where the dollhouse is?"

"No idea." When she fluttered her fingers, the fading rays of sunlight sparkled on a huge diamond. "And so, Cody, you won't bring Rue to the reception. Are we understood?"

"No problem," he said. "We have other plans for tonight. Dinner at Chez Mona."

Rue gave a surprised little gurgle and tugged on his sleeve, pulling him away from her mother and her bodyguard. "Will you excuse us for a moment?"

She dragged him toward the church parking lot where two stretch limos awaited the wedding party. When she looked up at him, her eyes were cautious. "You don't have to take me out for a fancy dinner. We both know that the only reason you asked me out in the first place was to establish a bond so you could get close to Danny."

Her reminder of his sleazy motive shamed him. Clearly, he was a rat bastard. "Things have changed."

"Yeah," she said. "We're already bonded. Way bonded."

"I want to take you someplace special." He had never been more sincere in his life. "I want to see candlelight in your hair and feed you oysters. I want to hear you giggle from too much champagne."

She glided her fingertips down his lapels and straightened his silk necktie. "Lovely as that sounds, we might still be in danger."

Yesterday, he would have thought she was being paranoid. But not after the attack at the construction site. "Change of plans," he said. "We'll pick up dinner from Chez Mona. I'll introduce you to the chef, and we'll eat at my place."

"Perfect."

He glanced back toward the church. "Since we're not going to the reception, we need to act fast after the ceremony. I want to talk to Jerome Samuels."

"I saw somebody else I want to chat with," she said. "His name is Mike Blanco."

Cody recalled the name from his research on his father's murder. "Another former cop?"

"He stayed on the force long after Danny and Uncle Bob left to do other things. They were buddies, called themselves the three amigos. I haven't seen Blanco in years. I'm sorry to say, he doesn't look healthy."

Blanco might be a good person to give him inside information on the police scandal. "I'd like to meet him, too. He probably knew my dad."

The screech of bagpipes split the air as the church doors opened. Leticia had vanished into the crowd, and Mel silently moved closer to Rue.

Cody gave her a wink and took off to find Jerome. He wasn't difficult to locate. For one thing, Jerome was as tall as Cody, four inches over six feet. Also, Jerome Samuels also seemed to be looking for him.

They met with a handshake and Jerome pulled him aside, "If I were you, I'd stay away from Danny. He blames you for putting Rue in danger last night."

"I appreciate the warning." Though Cody planned to ignore it.

"He's not happy about you and Rue hooking up." Jerome didn't show the least bit of hesitation about handling Danny's personal business. Apparently, his job as campaign manager went deeper than arranging political events. He was an enforcer. A lieutenant in Mayor Danny's army. "You should back off. Know what I mean?"

"I don't."

"We all know you're using her. Rue is cute, but she's not your type."

The aspersion ticked him off. Jerome was close enough to Danny to be part of Rue's family. He shouldn't be putting her down. "She's the most amazing woman I've ever known."

Jerome arched a disbelieving eyebrow. "Rue?"

"She's smart and talented. And beautiful. Did you know that her eyes change colors with her moods?" Cody stopped himself before he started talking about how sexy Rue was, how she purred, how her body responded to his touch like a finely tuned instrument. "You can tell Danny that I'm with Rue because there's nowhere else I'd rather be."

Jerome shrugged. "Why the hell did you take her to that construction site?"

"We were following up on the lousy job the cops are doing on this investigation."

"What do you mean?" A scowl creased his tanned forehead. "They already caught the guy."

Of all the things he could have said, this was the least expected. With an effort, Cody kept his expression impassive. "They're still holding Madigan? Even after what happened last night? After their eyewitness was killed?"

"That's right."

"On what evidence? Did they get fingerprints off the gun?"

"Not even a partial print. The gun and the bullets were wiped clean. Very professional."

"What else have they got on Madigan?"

The crowd gathered at the entrance to the church cheered and threw handfuls of birdseed as the bride and groom appeared. Jerome turned toward the celebration. "I should find my girlfriend."

Cody wouldn't let him go. He needed more information on the police investigation, and Detective Abbott wasn't sharing. "Help me out, Jerome. You know why I'm interested in this case."

"The link to your father's murder."

"You know what it's like." Cody appealed to the other man's history as a gang member. "You know how it feels to lose someone close to you."

"My sister." His lips tightened. "Killed in a drive-by. She was collateral damage."

"I'm sorry."

Turning away from the church, they walked together along the sidewalk, passing the smokers who were already lighting up.

After the mention of his sister, Jerome's attitude had changed. His jaw was tight. "I knew your father. Lucky Ted Berringer."

"Twenty years ago," Cody said. "You were a kid."

"Fourteen. Old enough to get into serious trouble. Back then, I was in a gang. Lucky Ted was with the DA's office. That made him the enemy."

"I get it." Cody didn't like having his father cast as the bad guy, but he appreciated Jerome's honesty.

"The cops pinned his murder on the gangs. Just like they made us responsible for every damn crime in the city. Drugs, rape, hookers, everything. It wasn't always true."

"In the case of my father's murder," Cody said. "Are you saying he *wasn't* murdered by the gangs?"

"I don't know. The guy he was supposed to meet at that warehouse was a badass. A killer."

"But he was also a snitch. My father was there to offer him a deal. It doesn't make sense for him to want my father dead."

"Doesn't matter. The snitch turned up dead." Jerome stopped walking and faced him. "It's been twenty years. You should move on."

"I can't ignore the facts," Cody said. "A murder weapon that was missing for twenty years has surfaced. And that Colt .45 was used in another murder. Why the hell aren't the police taking that seriously?"

"Because Madigan is the killer."

Circular logic. "Why are they so damn sure?"

"I shouldn't tell you this." Jerome glanced down the sidewalk to the wedding mob. "Madigan has done professional hits, and he got a fifty-thousand-dollar payoff two days before the murder. The detectives haven't traced the source yet, but they will."

Finally! A piece of tangible evidence. Cody appreciated the information. "I'd like to hear anything else you can tell me."

"Will you back off on your investigation?"

"Can't do it," Cody said. "Not while the real killer is gunning for Rue."

"If you really care about her, keep her out of sight. She couldn't identify the killer and shouldn't be a threat. Not to Madigan or anybody else. Sit back and wait for the case to go cold."

"Like with my father." He couldn't stand to have another unsolved case hanging over his head. "Do you remember anything else about him?"

Jerome unconsciously straightened his necktie. "I liked the way he dressed. Lucky Ted always used to wear a gold shamrock tiepin."

Cody tensed. He watched as Jerome's features fell into a bland expression. A cold breeze ruffled his blond hair. His eyes were blank. Had Jerome sent him the anonymous package containing the bumper sticker and shamrock tiepin?

"Is there anything else you want to tell me?" Cody asked.

"Can't think of a thing."

But Cody got the unspoken message. Jerome knew more than he was saying about the murder of Lucky Ted Berringer. And of Lindahl. And Tyler Zubek.

As the wedding crowd dispersed to their cars, Rue found herself face to face with Danny. She could tell that he was angry with her. Angry and disappointed.

No one else would have noticed the slight lift of

his eyebrows or the thinning of his lips as his teeth drew back in a grin. But she knew.

She'd seen that look before when she brought home a report card with less than perfect grades. And again in Little League when she struck out in the bottom of the ninth inning. She hated striking out.

Though she wasn't really his daughter, Rue had spent several years reading his every expression. Her mission in life had been to win Danny's approval. She still cherished that special day in Little League when he'd assigned her to play third base because she had the best arm on the whole team. She could make the double-play throw from third to first. A winner, Danny called her a winner. But that was a long time ago.

As she hugged him, she whispered, "I'm sorry about last night."

"It's okay," he whispered back. "I'm sure you wouldn't have done such a foolish thing if Cody hadn't pushed you into it."

"He didn't."

"Come on, now," he chastised. "I know guys like Cody. Smooth talkers. He wanted to play investigator and dragged you along."

"I'm not so easily manipulated."

"You're sweet-natured. That's what I like about—"

"It was my idea," she interrupted. "I was the one who wanted to talk to Tyler. I called his mother and found out where he was."

"Why the hell would you do something like that?"

"The police said they had the killer in custody."

"They do," Danny said. "They have the right man. Madigan is the killer."

His gaze linked with hers. He was persuasive enough to convince the entire city to vote for him as mayor, but she didn't believe him. Danny was lying to her.

"If Madigan is the killer, who shot Tyler?"

"I'm afraid that young Tyler Zubek was involved with some other criminal activity. There's no connection between his death and Lindahl's."

Except that Tyler was a witness. Just like she was a witness. "If you believe that, why did you call Mel to come back as a bodyguard?"

"Because you've witnessed another murder."

"By a killer who wore *exactly* the same hooded sweatshirt and drove *exactly* the same kind of car as the man who killed Lindahl."

"Coincidence," Danny said. "This kind of stuff happens all the time, honey. And it's not something you need to worry about."

Not unless the killer in the hooded sweatshirt picked her out as victim number three. "I can't just sit back and wait for—"

"Leave it alone, Rue. Let the police do their job."

Beyond Danny's left shoulder, she spotted Mike Blanco. He looked unwell. He'd always been skinny, but now he was skeletal. In contrast to Danny whose hair was still fiery red, Mike was completely gray.

She waved to him. "Mike Blanco. I haven't seen you in ages."

He took her hand in both of his. His touch was icy. "You've grown into a fine woman. Married?"

"Not yet." Dragging through her memory, she recalled that Mike had been married and divorced. There was one child. "How's your son?"

"He's not married, either. Lives back east near his mother. I hope to see him at Christmas."

When Danny enveloped his old friend in a politician's hug, she watched Blanco's face. No smile. Very little expression at all. He was carefully holding back.

And so was Danny.

It made sense to her that Blanco would be bitter about Danny's success. They had both started as beat cops and now seemed to be at opposite ends of the spectrum. Every bland word they spoke to each other was weighted with shared history and recrimination.

Blanco said, "A shame about Lindahl."

"The cops have his killer in jail," Danny said. "Two witnesses picked him out of a lineup."

"But not Rue." Blanco turned his pale gaze on her. His skin was as gray as his hair; he seemed to be fading into nothingness. "You couldn't identify the man in the lineup."

His tone was accusatory and, at the same time, questioning. Like a police interrogation. Even though Blanco was retired, he was still a cop.

"I didn't see him well," she said. "And I was scared."

"That's not the way I heard it. You picked up the gun and chased the perp down the street."

"Not the smartest thing I've ever done." She

shrugged. "Anyway, I didn't see much of his face. He had on a hooded sweatshirt and dark glasses. And his nose was weird. I wouldn't be surprised if it was fake."

"But those other two witnesses saw through the disguise." Blanco made a clicking noise in the back of his mouth. "Interesting."

"Good solid police work," Danny said firmly. "They've got the right guy. I'm sure of it. I wouldn't let Bob Lindahl's death go unpunished."

"I guess you wouldn't," Blanco said. "You boys were tight."

"We all were. All three of us. You, me and Lindahl."

His hearty tone was so phony that Rue felt embarrassed for him. She quickly changed the subject. "Speaking of Lindahl, I remember a dollhouse he built for me when I was a kid. Danny, do you know where it is?"

"Probably tucked away in the attic. I'll find it for you. Stop by the house tomorrow."

When Cody joined them, Mike Blanco came close to a real smile as he shook Cody's hand and said, "The son of Lucky Ted Berringer. I knew your father. He was a good man. Isn't that right, Danny?"

"A good man," Danny echoed as he stepped closer to Cody. "I don't want to hear about you putting Rue in danger again."

She couldn't believe his patronizing, bullying attitude. Hadn't she already explained to Danny that the decision to find Tyler Zubek was hers? Why was he being such a jerk?

"Rue is safe with me," Cody said coolly. "I care about what happens to her."

Mike Blanco cackled. "Ain't this something! The son of Lucky Ted and Danny's stepdaughter hooking up. Who'd have thunk it?"

And why was that so strange?

Chapter Eleven

Though Rue would have enjoyed attending the Scottish wedding reception where she could hear all the kudos and applause for her four-tiered tartan cake masterpiece, she was happier to be with Cody. *He cares about what happens to me*. He'd said so out loud, and she had every reason to believe him. Their lovemaking last night had been amazing, and she was hoping that tonight would be even better.

Being with him was exactly where she wanted to be. Unfortunately, they weren't alone. Not yet, anyway.

Mel the bodyguard accompanied them as they rode in the elevator to the thirty-fifth floor of a downtown Denver office building. This was where Cody's law firm was located, and he wanted to use his office computer to access information on Mike Blanco's history—financial and otherwise.

Behind her back, she heard Mel humming the "Wedding March."

"Knock it off," Cody muttered.

"Sorry. It's stuck in my head."

"That tune is a spike through the brain."

"What do you have against weddings?" she asked.

"Oh look," he said. "Here we are on the thirty-fifth floor already. Since it's Saturday, there shouldn't be many people in the office." He glanced back at Mel. "There's a built-in metal detector at the door, so you and your Glock will have to wait outside until I buzz you in."

"If it's all the same to you," Mel said, "I'll wait out here by the elevators."

Beside the carved oak double doors was a gold plaque that read: Taylor and Tomlinson, Attorneys at Law. Cody pressed his thumb against a tastefully hidden pad, and the lock clicked.

"Why all the security?" she asked.

"Corporate sharks have a lot of enemies."

He whisked her into the reception area with a long counter that matched the wood on the door. Plush burgundy chairs were arranged around a marble coffee table. In one corner stood a professionally decorated Christmas tree with silver and gold baubles. Though Rue wasn't a big fan of Remington's cowboy sculptures, she assumed the three-foot-tall bronze bronco and rider was an original and priceless. "Classy."

"Mostly for show. In negotiations, it's important to appear twice as successful as you really are."

"So if this place looks like a million bucks…"

"…it means I've had a very nice year."

He sauntered down the hall and turned to the left. His wasn't the corner office but right next door. It was a lot of square footage; her entire living room and dining room would fit inside these wainscoted walls. Even at dusk, the mountain view through a wall of windows was spectacular.

"No clutter," she noted.

"I have an efficient secretary."

Though she'd known that he was a hotshot eligible bachelor, the fact didn't really sink in until she saw him here in his looks-like-a-million-bucks office. Cody was more than just another attorney. He was hugely successful. He had it all.

He sloughed off his overcoat and went to a computer station against the wall. Flexing his fingers, he lowered his hands to the keys like a concert pianist starting a Mozart concerto. "Let's see what we can find about Michael Blanco. I don't suppose you know his middle name or address."

"He gave me his card." She dug into her purse, pulled out the plain white card with black script and read the Englewood address. "I think it's the same place where he lived years ago. It's probably paid off by now."

"Or refinanced," Cody said cynically.

She circled his tidy teak desk and slid into the buttery-soft leather chair. "What can you find out from the computer?"

"The basics, like employment history and credit rating. Then I can link into other info, like travel, major purchases, club memberships, any mention of his name in the newspaper or other articles. You'd be surprised how much information is out there."

"Is this legal?"

He nodded. "It's the same kind of program used by private investigators."

"Is this computer program how you found out that Bob Lindahl was heavily mortgaged?"

"That's right."

While he clicked away at the keys, she leaned back in the chair and propped her heels on his desk. Was this how corporate hotshots felt? She felt a sudden urge to buy out a midsized oil company. *Power.* Her mother had always said it was an aphrodisiac.

Rue remembered something else her mother had said. "How did Lindahl get the initial money to finance his construction business?"

Cody swiveled around in his chair to face her. "Why do you ask?"

"It must have taken a lot of cash to get started—way more than he could save up on a policeman's salary. Maybe Lindahl was involved in the bribery scandal."

Cody left the computer and came toward her. Bracing his hands on the arms of the chair, he leaned close. "What do you know about the police scandal?"

"Not much."

As she gazed up at him, thoughts of the investigation faded. God, he was handsome. It wasn't fair for a man to have such blue eyes, such long lashes. She wished that he'd do one of those dramatic gestures, sweeping his desk clean with one stroke and making love to her on the polished teak surface.

"My father," he said, "was investigating a group of cops who were taking bribes to look the other way on drug trafficking and gang violence."

"Did he investigate Lindahl?"

"He was cleared," Cody said. "Twenty years ago, flipping houses wasn't so common. But that's how Lindahl raised enough initial cash to draw in his investors."

"Of course." Lindahl's financials would have been the first thing Cody checked.

"How do you know about the scandal?" he asked. "Did Danny ever talk about it?"

She thought back to when she was a little girl. She'd been a quiet kid, always watching and listening. "I remember that he and my mom talked about money. Often and loudly."

"Did they argue?"

"There was never enough to suit Leticia." Rue had hated the tension between her parents. Terrified of losing her stepfather, she'd blocked out a lot of unpleasant memories. "Twenty years ago, I was only six. Just a kid. There's not much I recall."

"Any names? Or places?"

"Give me a hint. If I heard some of those names, they might ring a bell."

"Not a fair test," he said. "I'd be planting a suggestion in your mind. These have to be *your* memories."

She thought back to baseball games and birthday

parties and Christmas presents. For the most part, they were happy remembrances. "I only recall the good stuff."

"It's okay." He leaned closer and lightly kissed her lips. Her heart fluttered inside her ribcage. Her hands glided up his arms to his shoulders and she held him.

His smile warmed her from the inside out. His voice was husky as he said, "I can't wait to get you home and into bed."

"Finish up with your computer and let's go."

As he resumed his position at the keyboard, she leaned back and closed her eyes, anticipating tonight. In his bed. At his condo.

From the hallway, she heard the voices of other T&T employees who'd come in on the weekend. Probably it was a good thing that they weren't making love on his desktop.

After a few minutes, he swiveled around in the chair to face her. "Here's the story on Blanco. He put in twenty years on the police force and retired with a pension. Never rose high in the ranks. He mostly did desk work, overseeing the evidence room."

"He might know something about the gun."

Cody shook his head. "The weapon that killed my father was never found."

"What if it was? What if the gun was tucked away in a box somewhere in the evidence room?"

Though Cody's expression was skeptical, he said, "It gives us a reason to talk to Blanco."

She stood and went toward him, peering over his

shoulder at the computer screen. "Does it say anything about Blanco's health?"

"Bad ticker. He's had a couple of heart attacks."

Which explained his frail appearance. She felt
sorry for him. His two buddies had done very well
for themselves while he was stuck in a boring desk
job. Then his health failed. "Did he ever remarry?"

"Once. It lasted less than a year and there were no
kids. His only child—a son—is twenty-two and goes
to school in Fort Collins."

"That can't be right." Blanco had told her that his
son lived back east with his mother. "Are you sure
his son is local?"

Cody brought up the record on the computer
screen and pointed to it. Roger Blanco was a student,
majoring in veterinary sciences.

Why would a father lie about where his son lived?
What was Mike Blanco trying to hide?

AFTER THEIR STOP at Chez Mona where Rue met the
chef, Cody took her home to his condo. They were safe
enough on the seventeenth floor of this high security
building that they could dismiss Mel for the evening.

While she set out the fancy French dinner, he
changed into a pair of jeans and a crew-neck sweater.
Comfortable clothes for a comfortable evening. He
felt completely at home with Rue, possibly more so
than with his own family. In fact, he might even trust
her enough to take an unprecedented step: opening up
the Lucky Ted file and his private scrapbook.

A big step. Never before had he shared these details with anyone else. His grief was private and, somehow, sacred. But he wanted her to know *everything* about him. The good, the bad and the ugly. Plus, there was a practical reason—these details from his past might jog some of her buried memories.

When he came out of his bedroom and into the dining room, she'd set two places at his table. She'd turned the track lighting on low and lit some candles.

"You found my good china," he noticed.

"And your crystal." She picked up a wine goblet and pinged the edge. "I'll let you choose the wine."

Though he kept very little food around the house, his wine selection was decent. "White or red?"

"Something that goes with Chicken Kiev, escargots, baby spinach salad with extra virgin olive oil dressing, and the creamiest potatoes I've ever seen."

Her enthusiasm made him grin. "The way you love food, I'm amazed that you stay so slim."

"High metabolism," she said. "I burn it off."

"I know you're hot." He slipped an arm around her tiny waist. "Very hot."

She darted away from him. "First, we eat. I've already nuked this food once and I don't want to ruin the flavor by reheating it again."

From his temperature-controlled wine cabinet in the kitchen, he selected a California shiraz. Opening it with a corkscrew, he glanced out the windows. Light snow had begun to fall in pale gusts that blurred the lights and hid the stars. By tomorrow, the city would look like Christmas.

He poured the wine and sat down to an excellent dinner. The rich flavors excited his palate, but the real treat was watching Rue as she chewed slowly and savored every bite. Damn, she was sexy with her little moans of pleasure and the way she licked her lips.

"Heavy cream," she murmured, "makes everything taste better. There's another ingredient in these potatoes, something I can't quite identify."

"Vanilla," he said. Like the subtle fragrance that surrounded her.

"I think you're right." She wrinkled her forehead in concentration as she took another taste. "Definitely vanilla. And I am definitely stuffed."

"You didn't clean your plate."

"That's the thing with French food. The sauces are so rich that you can't eat too much." Exhaling a contented sigh, she leaned back in her chair and gazed out at the falling snow. "When it's cold outside, it feels so good to be all warm and cozy."

"Do you ski?"

"Not very well," she admitted. "I don't get up to the mountains often. Managing the cake business sucks up all of my time."

"We should take a long weekend. Maybe in January. I could have my secretary make reservations at this little bed-and-breakfast in Breckenridge."

"I'll clear my schedule," she said with a snap of her fingers.

He sipped his wine, aware that he was making plans for next month. A commitment. How the hell could he know if they'd still be together in January? Mentally, he slammed on the brakes. Cody knew better.

Too many things could go wrong between them, starting with her loyalty to Danny. If their investigation pointed toward her former stepfather, Rue would have to choose between them, and he didn't think he'd come out on top.

He rose from the table. It was time to show his hand. If he expected her to open up to him, he had to trust her with his secrets.

"Come with me, Rue. There's something in my office that I want to show you."

Chapter Twelve

Though it was only a few paces from the dining table to Cody's home office, the distance felt like a ten-mile hike uphill. Rue didn't want to go back there. That office was the site of their most unpleasant moment.

This relationship—or whatever it was between her and Cody—had changed a lot since that first night when she'd stayed at his condo and peeked into his office. His desk had been strewn with clutter, and Cody had been deep in concentration. His sadness was palpable.

All she'd wanted to do was tell him that she was sorry, but he'd chased her down and accused her of spying. Then he'd tried to redeem himself with that phony kiss. As if he could make everything better with a little taste of his charisma? He'd deserved it when she'd slapped him. No regrets on her part.

When she entered his inner sanctum, the room itself didn't look the least bit menacing. Just a small office with a desk, a computer station and book-shelves. A quick glance at the spines showed several murder mystery novels mingled with reference works.

Cody went behind the desk. "I've never shown this to anyone else before."

When he smacked the side of a sturdy cardboard box, she jumped. "Why me?"

"Memories," he said. "I want you to try to remember the events of twenty years ago."

She couldn't imagine how her six-year-old perceptions could be of any practical use, but she was willing to keep an open mind. "What's in the box?"

"All the evidence I've collected over the years about my father's murder. Some of the notes he gathered on his investigation. Court briefs. Police documents. Newspaper clippings."

He paused to finish off his wine. Though his tone was matter-of-fact and calm, she knew that sharing these memories was difficult. He'd said that *no one* had seen the contents of this file before.

She felt privileged to be taken into his confidence. At the same time, she didn't want to disappoint him. "Suppose I remember something. How will that add to your information?"

"You have a different perspective. A different angle. You've already helped me notice things I hadn't looked at before."

"Such as?"

"Jerome Samuels. I never paid any attention to him. But he was there at the time, involved with gangs. Potentially a useful witness." He added, "And you gave me a new focus on Mike Blanco."

Though she still wasn't convinced that she'd be helpful, she couldn't refuse. Circling the desk, she sat in the chair. "Let's see what you've got."

Reaching into the box, he took out a battered scrapbook with a faded picture of the Rockies on the cover. He placed it on the desk in front of her and opened to the first page.

His right hand rested on the corner of the lined paper as if he hated to let go. She looked down at the strong wrist and long fingers of an adult, masculine hand. But the writing on this page was unformed, childlike. Cody had been twelve when he'd written this account of his father's funeral.

In his scribbled words, she saw the vulnerability that he kept so carefully hidden as an adult. She felt a wave of tenderness toward the young boy who had carefully written these lines in ink, making corrections with Wite-Out.

She asked, "Why haven't you ever shown this to anyone else?"

"I tried with my mother, and she told me to let it go. Leave the investigation to the police."

An echo of what Danny had said to her this afternoon. "Did you talk to the investigating officers?"

"They weren't interested in the homicide theories of a twelve-year-old kid." He stroked the page again. "This was my project. Mine alone. It gave me a certain amount of comfort to work on my scrapbook.

I used to dream about finding the killer and seeing him locked up behind bars."

She imagined him as a child, sitting alone in a house of mourning while he collected evidence and tried to make sense of tragedy.

Leaning over the scrapbook, she read his observations. The date of his father's funeral, written at the top of the page was June 23, 1987. Then he described the weather: clear and seventy-eight degrees.

His account was detailed and strangely lacking in emotion. Instead, he recorded the numbers: one hundred and eighty-two people attended. Seven floral displays decorated the altar, even though the family had requested no flowers. They had asked that donations be made to a homeless shelter.

"Hathaway House," she read. "That's the homeless shelter you were collecting for when you were dressed as Santa Claus."

"My mother's favorite charity," he said. "I host a benefit for them every year."

"Tell me the next time your benefit rolls around and I'll donate a cake."

"Just like that? Don't you want to know more about them?"

"Any charity that can keep a cynic like you involved must be doing good work."

She returned to the page. Because Lucky Ted was a veteran, there was a four-man marine honor guard. Twelve-year-old Cody made a note that he was holding his mother's Valium and she could only have two more pills before bedtime. He had to take care of things; he was the man of the house.

Touched by his account, she looked up at him. Behind his slick facade with his perfectly trimmed black hair and steely blue gaze, she saw a brave soul who had weathered devastating grief. Her heart filled with sympathy, but there was nothing she could say to heal his pain.

The only solution was to find his father's murderer. Toward that end, she searched her memories. "I remember that summer. Danny and my mother had been married for almost a year. He was coaching my Little League team."

"You've mentioned that before," he said. "The baseball team."

"A great confidence builder. Before Danny joined our family, I wasn't athletic. But it turned out that I had a good arm. Played third base because I was the only one on the team who could make the throw from third to first."

"Impressive," he said dryly.

"I was never really fast. Danny said I ran like a girl. Still do."

"That summer," he said, "Danny went to my father's funeral. He signed the guest book. There were several cops, including Lindahl and Blanco."

"Kind of surprising," she said, "since your father was investigating a police scandal."

"I think that's why so many officers showed up.

If they didn't attend, it was almost like an admission of guilt."

On the next page were yellowed newspaper articles about the murder, the crime scene and obituaries. Her gaze focused on two incredibly sad words: "survived by…" Lucky Ted had left behind his wife and five children, both parents, three sisters and their children. "You have a big family."

"When we all get together, it's epic. This last Thanksgiving was a free-for-all at one of my aunts' houses. Twenty adults and twice that many kids."

"Sounds like a Cecil B. DeMille production."

"What did you do for Thanksgiving?"

Here was something she didn't want to talk about. "The usual."

"Dinner with your mother?"

"She and the judge went out of town. They visited his daughter in San Francisco. She has a new baby."

Cody asked, "Did you go to Danny's house?"

Embarrassed to tell him how she'd spent the holiday, she flipped through another couple of pages of newspaper clippings. "Danny invited me."

"And you went to his house?"

She frowned. "Is this some kind of interrogation?"

"Just curious."

And she knew he wasn't going to drop the subject until she told him the whole story. It was only fair for her to come clean since he was sharing his innermost thoughts with her. "I had four invitations. With all my mother's marriages, I have more step-relations than

I know what to do with. But I'm not really part of any family unit. I'm an outsider. The quiet stepsister who's on everybody's list for Christmas cards and birth announcements even though they can't quite remember how they know me."

He leaned down beside her and held her chin so he could look deeply into her eyes. "You spent Thanksgiving alone."

No big deal. Frankly, she preferred her own company to dealing with uncomfortable situations where nobody cared about her or—even worse—took her under their wing as a fixer-upper. Tried to find her a husband. Get her settled with a family of her own.

"I didn't feel sad about it," she said. "Not until right this moment. Please tell me that you don't feel sorry for me."

"Why should I? Nothing wrong with being alone."

Though she and Cody came from different backgrounds, they shared much in common. "You're a loner, too."

"But I'd rather be with you."

His poignant kiss tasted as sweet as wine. She closed her eyes, welcoming the rush of tingling sensation that raised goosebumps on her arms and wiped away all other thought and logic. "More."

Too quickly, he moved away. "Later," he promised. "Right now, I want you to concentrate."

But she wanted to make love now. "This is a lot of information. You need to tell me what you're looking for."

"I have a time line."

From a separate file, he took out several sheets of graph paper taped together. The notations were color-coded in marker. "This first page is 1987, starting with June. My father was killed on the fourteenth. His body was found in a downtown warehouse where he was supposed to be meeting a gang informant. My notes on the informant are in red."

"What case was your father investigating?"

"The bribery scandal. The informant—a gang member—was going to give the names of the dirty cops in exchange for a deal."

"What kind of deal?" she asked.

Cody flipped back to the newspaper clippings in the scrapbook and pointed to the article. "He was picked up for dealing drugs and might have been involved in a drive-by shooting."

"Not a very credible witness," she said.

Cody pointed to the next dot on his time line. "Five days later, the police arrested some of the other members of the informant's gang."

She traced the line with her finger. "The funeral was on the twenty-third."

"And the informant—noted in red—was shot and killed on the thirtieth. The police were convinced that he had murdered my father. Case closed."

The investigation seemed open-and-shut, but Cody's time line extended far longer. She squinted at a notation in yellow. "What does this mean?"

"Yellow stands for a cop who was killed in the line of duty in August."

"I get it," she said. "All of these different colors are assigned to different people involved with the case."

"Right." He pointed to a note in turquoise. "This is Bob Lindahl. In February of 1989, he quit the force to start his construction company."

If Cody had made notes pertaining to Uncle Bob, he surely would have been following Danny's career. Silently, she studied the time line. Notations in green used the initials *DM* for Danny Mason.

There in black and white—or green and white—was the real reason Cody wanted her memories. He wanted her to remember details that might incriminate her former stepfather.

If he'd said from the start that he wanted information on Danny, she would have dismissed his suspicions as outrageous. But now that she saw his time line, she understood that Danny was only part of the case. Possibly, her memories could exonerate him.

She concentrated on the green notes. "In November, Danny was appointed to the gang task force." She skipped ahead on the time line. "One year after your father's death, there was a truce established with the gangs. And Danny was promoted."

"What do you remember about that time period?"

She slid an irritated glance in his direction. "Like an unexplained influx of cash that might have come from a bribe? Or secret meetings with criminals?"

"I'm not accusing Danny of anything," Cody said.

"But he was a big part of the action. Those gang negotiations kicked off his political career."

"I'm not going to be much help," she said. "My memories of Danny were tinged with hero worship. I loved being with him, tagging along."

"Do you remember Jerome Samuels?"

"Danny took a special interest in him. Which made me jealous. I hated anything that took Danny's attention away from me."

"And your ace throwing arm," he lightly teased. "In the winter when you weren't playing Little League, what kind of things did you and Danny do?"

"We went to the gym and watched the Golden Gloves boxers." A hint of memory teased the edge of her mind. "Big, scary guys. Stinky, too. One time, Danny got in the ring with this guy who had a snake tattoo curling up his arm."

"When was that?"

"September or November. The Bronco season had started, and I was wearing an Elway T-shirt. Lucky number seven."

In the back of her mind, she recalled the rumbling voices of men in the gym. She was tall enough to see over the first rope into the ring, but she kept her eyes closed because she didn't want to see Danny get hurt. "I was scared. They weren't wearing the protective headgear. Lindahl was there. And Blanco."

"Anybody else? Maybe Jerome?"

"I don't think so."

"I guess not," Cody said. "That fight was before

the gang negotiations started. Jerome wouldn't have been in the picture."

She looked down at the time line again. Her memory blurred around the edges. "Danny won. After he knocked his opponent down, he spat out his mouthpiece and pointed with his glove toward three men who were watching. 'Now we talk.' That's what Danny said."

"The stuff legends are made of." Cody took her hands and pulled her out of the desk chair and into his arms. "After that fist fight, gang negotiations got underway. And Danny had earned himself a place at the table."

"I never knew the fight was that important," she said.

"And I didn't really believe it happened."

"But it did. I was there." And Danny had been a hero. She was right to be proud of him, to believe in him. "Maybe now you can accept the truth. Danny had nothing to do with your father's murder."

"But someone close to him did."

She exhaled a frustrated sigh. Why wouldn't Cody give up? "How can you be so sure?"

"I'm not," he said as he wrapped his arms around her waist. "If I had the answers, I'd put my Lucky Ted files through the shredder."

"Then what? After you got done with the shredder, what would you do?"

"I'd move on," he said dryly. "I'd have the kind of closure that shrinks and grief counselors talk about."

"Cynical," she said, assessing his mood. "Have you been to therapists?"

"Not lately."

She placed her palms flat against his chest, then slid them down his torso. As far as she was concerned, the investigating portion of their evening was over. She was ready to move on to bigger and better things.

At the waistband of his jeans, she slid her hands inside his sweater, touching his bare flesh. Her fingers crawled across his muscular back as she pulled him tight against her.

He was already hard, ready to make love. The fluttering anticipation in her stomach distracted her, but she returned doggedly to the subject.

"You've spent most of your life looking for this killer," she said. "When you finally find him, there might be an empty space."

"You could help me fill it up," he said.

His warmth soaked into her. His arms were secure and comfortable. "I could start tonight," she offered.

"And tomorrow?"

"We'll visit Danny. And maybe Mike Blanco in the afternoon." She stared into his azure eyes. "Tonight is for us."

His first kiss took her breath away. By the second kiss, she'd managed to pull his crew-neck sweater up and over his shoulders.

He was naked from the waist up. His jeans hung low on his hips. His broad chest was sprinkled with black hair—soft and springy at the same time. She rubbed her cheek against the firm muscles. His totally masculine body fascinated and aroused her. She could explore him for hours, for days.

When he cupped her breast and kneaded, she felt intoxicated—drunk with sensual pleasure.

His kisses trailed down her throat, and she arched against him. She moaned. Her breath came in excited little gasps.

She couldn't wait to get into his bed.

Chapter Thirteen

Only half-awake, Cody dreamed that a nest of little yellow birds were perched on his brow, pecking steadily at his forehead. Reaching up, he brushed the birds away. *Birdbrain. I have birds on the brain.*

Then the pinging started again on his ear.

His eyelids pried open. The bedside lamp was lit. Rue hovered over him, flicking her finger at his earlobe. What the hell?

The clock said it was forty-seven minutes past five. Before dawn. On a Sunday.

"Finally," Rue said. "I thought you'd never get up."

"I'm not up." He rolled to his side, away from the light.

"Don't you dare go back to sleep."

He was vaguely aware that she was fully dressed, which meant no chance for wake-up sex. No reason to get out of his nice, warm, cozy bed.

"Come on," she urged as she climbed over his shoulder. She was the bird, the little yellow bird.

Annoying and cute at the same time. She chirped, "We have a lot to do today. We're going to Danny's house. Then later, we'll visit Mike Blanco."

"Neither of them can possibly be awake," he grumbled. "Sane people sleep late on Sunday."

"Get up." She pinched his naked butt.

"Ow."

"I need to bake a couple of cakes. One for Danny. One for Blanco. And then, there are all those orders for gingerbread houses."

She pinched again with her sharp little fingernails.

He'd had enough. He threw off the covers and leapt on top of her, pinning her arms to the sheets.

She shook her head, tossing her long hair out of her face. Her eyes were a dark green and determined. "Fine, Cody. You can sleep in if you want to, but—"

He silenced her with a kiss. Her token struggles subsided, and she went limp beneath him. Her chirpy demands faded into a sexy moan.

"This is the way I like you," he murmured. "All soft and willing."

"Wrong. I need to get moving." But her tone was far less defiant. "I'll go to the shop by myself and start baking."

He knew she'd do it. She'd charge out the door of his condo unprotected and vulnerable to any threat. "Take it easy, cupcake."

"Gotta get cooking. If I'm going to spend most of the day tracking down clues with you, I need to get caught up on my other work."

Her blue work shirt gaped open at the neck, revealing the creamy flesh above her breasts. He nuzzled her collarbone.

"Not now," she protested. "Sex later."

"Promise."

"Tonight," she said. "I'll make you glad you waited."

He had no doubt that she would. Releasing her arms, he collapsed on the bed beside her. "Five minutes' more sleep. Then we can go."

"It's really okay for you to sleep in. I can manage on my own."

With a growl, he hauled himself out of the bed and into the bathroom. He wouldn't make the mistake of leaving her open to danger.

Less than fifteen minutes later, they were in his car and on the way to Ruth Ann's Cakes. During the night, a few inches of snow had fallen. The streetlights reflected on a pristine white icing that coated the branches of trees and the roofs of houses.

The roads were icy, and he approached the corner stoplight with caution.

In the passenger seat, Rue rubbed her mittens together. "It finally looks like Christmas. Beautiful, white and clean."

"And dark," he muttered. "Who the hell gets up at this hour?"

"Bakers. Newspaper delivery people. Skiers who want an early start."

He hadn't really been asking for a list of all the

people who were active at the crack of dawn. Didn't care.

"Call Mel and tell him to meet us at your shop." He nodded to Rue. "Use my cell phone."

"Do we really need to wake him this early?"

"It's his job."

Protecting her was why Danny had hired a bodyguard. His intentions toward Rue seemed genuine and protective, but Cody had other questions for Danny Mason.

Rue's memories hadn't implicated him in any way. In fact, Danny was coming out as a hero who used his fists to initiate gang negotiations.

Cody was willing to accept that Danny Mason—the newly elected mayor of Denver—wasn't involved in his father's death, but he might have a clue to the identity of the killer. That might have been the intended message of the anonymous package containing Danny's bumper sticker and Lucky Ted's signature tiepin: Danny had the clue.

The small parking lot behind her shop was empty, as were the streets, in spite of Rue's insistence that lots of people were awake at this time of the morning. Nobody was around.

Inside the kitchen of her shop, Cody's cell phone rang. It was Mel. His car wouldn't start. Of course not. Life just got more and more annoying.

Cody ended the call and turned toward Rue. She'd already shed her jacket and slipped an apron over her blue work shirt.

"I've got to pick up Mel," he said. "His car won't start."

"You go ahead. I'll be okay."

"He's not far from here. I ought to be back in fifteen minutes."

"Not to worry." Birdlike, she cocked her head. "You said it yourself, Cody. There's nobody around at this hour. I'm perfectly safe."

Dawn wasn't the time for killers, and they hadn't seen anyone outside. No footprints or tire tracks. Still, he worried. "I wish you hadn't said that."

"Why?"

"In horror movies, the pretty girl always says she's perfectly safe just before the psycho attacks."

"This isn't a movie." She approached him, went up on tiptoes and kissed him. "Be careful driving."

Rue was tired of being scared, looking over her shoulder and wondering when the next attack would come. When Cody left, closing the door tightly behind himself, she took a deep breath and allowed the silence of her kitchen to settle around her.

Though the time she'd spent with him was better than Christmas morning, she appreciated a moment alone. Humming to herself, she went to the refrigeration unit and took out four pounds of butter and a cool container of heavy cream. For her visit to Danny's house, she'd make a simple chocolate cake with buttercream frosting—his favorite. The only decoration would be a couple of fancy swirls. And for Mike Blanco? Since he'd had a couple of heart attacks, she ought to stick to the low-cholesterol "Ruth-less" recipe. Maybe she should write something provocative across the top: the word *liar* in bright red. Blanco should have told the truth about his son going to college nearby.

She heard a knock on the back door. Had Cody forgotten something? She hurried across the kitchen, unfastened the lock and opened it.

Standing there, outlined by the light from the alley was the man in the hooded sweatshirt. He stuck out a gloved hand and shoved the door wider.

Shocked, she reacted. Darting across the kitchen, she ducked behind the counter.

"Wait," he said. His voice was a weirdly disguised falsetto. "I'm not going to hurt you."

Breathing hard, fighting panic, she stared at him. The hood on his pea-green sweatshirt covered his head. He wore sunglasses. The lower portion of his face was covered with a black scarf. There was no way she could possibly identify him.

There was something familiar about him. The set of his shoulders? The way he stood? His posture was hunched over so she couldn't even guess at his height.

"I came to warn you," he said. "It's Danny. He's dangerous."

"You killed Tyler Zubek."

"No," he said. "Somebody else got to him. Somebody who wouldn't pay his price. Danny. It was Danny. He hired the killer."

"Why?"

She couldn't believe she'd asked him a question. Yet that was what you were supposed to do. Engage your attacker in conversation, make him see you as a real person. Did those lessons apply to professional hit men?

"Tyler threatened to change his eyewitness identification, and Danny couldn't have that. Danny wants this case closed. No more investigation."

"But you were there. You shot at us."

"Sorry."

Had he really apologized to her? This was too bizarre. "If you're so innocent," she said, "why don't you turn yourself in as a witness?"

"Can't trust the cops. They work for Danny."

He took a step closer, and she backed away. Her knives were close at hand. But she couldn't risk being close enough to stab him. He wasn't innocent. She'd seen him fire three bullets into Uncle Bob's chest. "You killed Bob Lindahl."

"He had it coming." The falsetto cracked. "Tell Danny to pay. And nobody else gets hurt. Not you. Not anybody."

He took another step.

She couldn't let him come closer. Even though he appeared to be of average size, she knew he could overpower her.

Reaching down to the counter, she grabbed a pound of butter. With the strong right arm of a third baseman, she fired the butter at him. He ducked.

With another pound of butter, she threw again. And again.

Backing up, she was at the refrigeration unit. After throwing the last pound of butter, she darted inside and closed the door.

It was a small space and chilly, of course. But she didn't feel the cold; her racing blood kept her warm. She could get out of here at any time. There was a safety handle on the inside of the door. And he could get in.

She flicked on the overhead light and searched for weapons. No knives in here. But there was ice cream. French vanilla and chocolate. Two heavy containers—five pounds each. She grabbed one off the shelf and set it at her feet. The other she raised up high. God, it was heavy. She rested the cardboard drum on her head, ready to throw. If he opened the door, she'd hit him with the ice cream. When he was down, she'd run.

A frightened sob escaped her lips. Cody had been right. This was a horror movie.

The minutes ticked by like hours. How long had she been in here? Did she dare to open the door?

Cody would be back soon. And Mel would be with him. What if they walked into an ambush?

The man in the sweatshirt had said he didn't want to hurt her. His enemy was Danny. He'd said Danny was responsible for Tyler's death. That couldn't be true.

Her arms ached from holding the five-gallon tub. Her fingers were freezing. What kind of payment did the man in the sweatshirt want from Danny? It had to be blackmail. For what? Something in the past. Lucky Ted's murder? Did Danny have something to do with the murder of Cody's father?

She'd fought this suspicion from the moment Cody had raised it. Danny was one of the good guys. He was the closest thing she had to a father. Not a murderer, he couldn't be a murderer.

The door opened. Before she threw the ice cream, she recognized Cody. Dropping the tub of French vanilla, she flew into his arms. "Is he gone?"

"Nobody's here." Cody held her against his chest. "What the hell happened?"

"The guy in the sweatshirt. He had a scarf over his face. I can't identify him."

Over his shoulder, he called to Mel. "The killer was here. Search the place."

He held her close, and she snuggled against his chest as the warmth returned to her body. They should call the police and put them on the trail. But why bother? *Danny controls the police.* She knew that to be true. Danny was the newly elected mayor; he had influence.

"Are you okay?" Cody asked.

"I'm not hurt."

Though she was in his arms, she felt herself pulling away, retreating into a protective shell. She didn't want to tell him what the man in the sweatshirt had said about Danny. It was all lies, and she didn't want to get Cody started in the wrong direction.

"How did he get in here?"

"I opened the door," she said. "It was only a minute

after you left. When I heard the knock, I thought you were coming back for something you'd forgotten."

Instead of chastising her, he rubbed her shoulders and back as if she'd fallen into a freezing bath and he needed to start her circulation. "Tell me what happened, Rue."

She couldn't lie to him. Cody had been kind and protective and more. They were intimate; he was her lover. If she allowed her emotions free rein, she had to admit that the way she felt about him came close to love. She had to tell Cody the truth.

But she couldn't betray Danny.

She couldn't choose between these two men.

A frustrated tear slipped from her eyelid and coursed down her cheek. She pressed her face against his chest and whispered, "He had a warning."

"About what?"

She lied, "He wants us to quit investigating."

Though she couldn't see Cody's face, she felt the tension in his hands. His breathing tightened. "Not a bad idea. It seems like I can't keep you safe. I'm not used to looking over my shoulder, anticipating the next assault. I don't think like a cop."

"We can't quit now." Not while she had these unanswered questions about Danny. She couldn't spend the rest of her life wondering. "The warning means we're on the right track. We're going to find your father's murderer."

Even if the killer was Danny?

Chapter Fourteen

By midafternoon the sun had come out, melting last night's snow to a wet slush on the roads. Only a thin coating of white covered the lawns in Danny's residential neighborhood where Christmas candy canes, wreaths and plastic Santas had become part of the architecture.

Cody glanced toward Rue who stared straight ahead with both hands on the steering wheel of her van. Her long hair flowed softly around her shoulders, but she was obviously tense.

She'd been like that all day. Demanding. Stubborn. Working at her baking like a woman possessed. She wouldn't allow him to report the early-morning attack to the police and dismissed the danger with a flip comment about how the cops couldn't do anything. A couple of times, he'd caught her staring at him and then quickly looking away, refusing to meet his eyes.

She sure as hell wasn't the same woman who'd

engaged with him in last night's sexual gymnastics. In bed, she'd been open and inventive. Today, she was closed off, secretive. No Trespassing signs were posted at her borders.

Even Bernice had noticed Rue's tension. She'd warned Cody, "She's in quite a mood."

"How do I fix it?" Cody had asked.

"You don't." Bernice had narrowed her eyes under iridescent green eyelids that matched her skintight turquoise outfit. Her mermaid look. "You just try to stand clear when she erupts."

Cody could feel that explosion coming. They were only a few blocks away from the house that Danny shared with his new wife, Elaine, and her two young children from a former marriage. Supposedly, they were here to pick up the dollhouse made for Rue by Bob Lindahl.

He asked, "Why is this dollhouse so important to you?"

"It was part of my childhood," she said tersely.

"Lighten up, Rue."

"What?" She pulled over to the curb and parked. He imagined Mel—who was following in his own car—screeching to a halt. "What did you say?"

"You've been snarling like a wet cat."

"Oh, this is terrific." She threw up her hands. "Mr. Dark-and-Brooding is advising *me* to be more cheerful."

Stand clear. She's about to blow. "Maybe if you told me what was wrong, I could..."

"Do what? Fix my whole life?" She strained against her seat belt. "Wave your magic wand and make my mother stay married to the same person? Great idea, Cody. While you're at it, maybe you can turn Danny into the perfect father figure I always imagined he was."

He'd never heard her say anything against Danny before. "What did Danny do?"

Her forehead pinched. Her teeth bared. *Fire in the hole*. He could almost smell the lava. "Danny abandoned me. Just like my real father. And all the other fathers that came after him. I know they were divorcing Leticia, but they dumped me, too."

Shutting the door and leaving her out in the cold. There wasn't anything Cody could say to comfort her; she was right. Her sole definition of what a family was supposed to be had been wrapped up in Danny. And that was one seriously flawed definition.

She dashed away her tears as they fell. "Okay," she said more quietly. "Okay, I'm fine."

"Let's forget about the dollhouse and go home to my place."

"Do you know what really hurt? When Danny was campaigning, Jerome asked me not to be involved. I didn't fit into the picture of his perfect family."

"Who needs Danny? You fit into my picture just fine."

She almost smiled. "Let's get this over with."

She deserved a hell of a lot better life than the one she'd gotten, and Cody had an idea of how he could make things better for her. He flipped open his cell phone and made a quick phone call.

They pulled up to the curb outside a two-story, brick Tudor-style house. Nice place. Big yard. Suitable for Denver's next mayor.

Cody's plan was to get a few minutes alone with Danny. In spite of Jerome's warning that Danny didn't like him, Cody had a couple of questions about what had happened twenty years ago, and Danny had the answers.

As he and Rue walked up the winding sidewalk, Danny threw open the door and welcomed them. He seemed warm and open—an attitude that could be attributed to a politician's knack for being everybody's best friend.

His wife was a skinny blond woman who dutifully kissed Rue's cheek, shook Cody's hand and offered hot chocolate to go with the fancy two-layer cake Rue had brought for the family.

Cody turned down the cocoa but accepted when Danny mentioned grown-up drinks in the den. Leaving the women and Mel to deal with the cake, he and Danny passed a ceiling-high Christmas tree and entered a masculine room with heavy furniture. A bay window looked out on the backyard where a plastic reindeer with big eyes and a red nose lurked in the spruce trees.

Danny muttered, "This is the only room in the house without decorations. The wife threatened to put a cutesy Grinch in here. I told her if she did, I'd shoot the damn thing's head off."

"Had enough of Christmas?"

"Hell, yes." He went to a wet bar in the corner of the room and took down a bottle of brandy. "I posed for the photogs while I flipped the light switch for the City and County Building. Next week, I'll ride a float in the Parade of Lights. And I had to go to church this morning and hear about how we all should give money to a relief fund rather than buying presents. It's all too warm and fuzzy for me. I'm looking forward to the real work of government. Education. Tax breaks for the tourist board."

"Law and order," Cody said.

"That's right." He poured two tumblers half full. "You're a savvy guy. I don't need to tell you that I want this mess with Lindahl to go away."

"You think Madigan is the killer."

"Damn right, I do. He's a professional hit man."

Cody accepted the tumbler of brandy. "Who hired him?"

"He'll tell the cops. Sooner or later, Madigan will figure out that he can save himself a couple of years in prison if he gives up the person who hired him." Danny took a healthy swig from his glass and checked his wristwatch and muttered, "Less than an hour from now, I'm supposed to watch preschoolers singing carols at the mall."

Cody got the message. Time was short. He couldn't bother with subtlety. "Madigan used the same gun that killed my father. That's a clear message. The truth about Lindahl's murder is tied up in the past."

"Twenty years ago," Danny said. "A long time. I can't even remember what I had for breakfast this morning."

Cody wasn't about to let him off the hook. "You were there. You weren't in homicide, but you were a rising star on the force."

"I was just a cop. Like everybody else."

His modesty rang false. "I sure as hell hope you were different. Twenty years ago, a lot of cops were corrupt."

"According to Lucky Ted," Danny snapped back. "Those charges never stuck."

"I don't give a damn about who was on the take twenty years ago." Cody sipped the brandy without tasting it. "I want to find the man who killed my father."

Danny's shoulders squared; his posture was adversarial. They weren't wearing boxing gloves, but this was definitely a sparring match. "Some people said Lucky Ted was too smart for his own good. Don't make the same mistake."

"Being too smart?"

"Not knowing when to back off."

A threat? "He had evidence on the dirty cops."

"Circumstantial," Danny shot back.

"Too many instances of gross negligence on cases involving the gangs. The police made mistakes, and the bad guys walked. Time after time."

"Doesn't mean a damn thing." Danny's jaw stuck out. "You don't know what it's like to be a cop. It's the front lines. Danger on every street corner. Your father didn't understand that."

"Yet, he was killed."

Danny's mouth twisted in a sneer. "What's this really about? Some kind of accusation?"

"Only a question." Cody didn't expect Danny to rat on his buddies or to confess about bribes he might have taken. "You were there. You know things I can only guess about."

Danny drew himself up. "Go ahead and ask."

"According to all the reports, my father went to that warehouse alone and unarmed. Why?"

"He was supposed to be meeting a snitch," Danny said with a shrug. "Obviously, he didn't expect trouble."

"The set-up had ambush written all over it. A deserted warehouse? Late at night? And the snitch wasn't a Boy Scout. He was a gang member who was involved in a drive-by shooting."

"Your father screwed up. It wouldn't be the first time that a bright-eyed DA made the mistake of trusting a snitch."

Cody put forth his own theory. "My father wasn't a fool and he wouldn't have gone to that meeting alone. I think he *had* backup. A cop."

Danny tilted back his head and drained the dregs of his brandy. "Based on what evidence?"

"Logic," Cody said. "It only makes sense that my father would have gone to the warehouse with somebody he trusted—trusted with his life. Somebody who was supposed to protect him but looked the other way when he was shot and killed."

"And you think I know who it was."

The mere fact that Danny hadn't dismissed his theory spoke volumes. Cody was on the right track. "I think you do."

"If I had evidence, I would have spoken up twenty years ago."

"Somebody knows," Cody said. "Somebody used that murder weapon on Lindahl to send a message."

Danny checked his wristwatch. "I'm out of time."

"Was it Lindahl?" Cody took a stab. "Did he fail to protect my father twenty years ago and then get himself killed by the same weapon?"

"If you think I'm going to dump suspicion on my dead friend, you're crazy." Danny came toward him and jabbed an angry forefinger at his face. He was so close that Cody could see the tracery of broken blood vessels across his ruddy cheeks. "You need to forget about this."

He wished Danny would touch him and give him a reason to strike back. "I can't forget."

"Leave it to the cops. It's over. Your father's murder isn't going to be solved. Not now. Not ever. Let the man rest in peace."

"Not until I know who killed him. I want justice."

"You want revenge," Danny said. "Cold, ugly revenge. And you're using my stepdaughter for your own agenda."

"I didn't put her on the scene. I didn't make her an eyewitness to Lindahl's murder."

"Neither did I." Abruptly, he backed off. "I wish like hell that she wasn't involved."

Finally, they were in agreement. Both of them were concerned about Rue's safety. That was the only thing they had in common.

IN THE family room of Danny's ornate house, Rue sipped gooey sweet hot chocolate and watched as Danny's stepchildren played with the dollhouse. Ages six and eight, a boy and a girl, they were incredibly adorable. Both blond with Wedgwood-blue eyes.

"It's a lovely dollhouse," their mother said. "So detailed."

And it's mine. Selfishly, Rue wanted to snatch the miniature house away and carry it off with her. This should have been *her* childhood—neat and pretty, surrounded with twinkling Christmas lights and a loving family. Though Danny and his new wife, Elaine, probably argued as much as he and Leticia had, there was no sign of marital strife. They were picture-perfect. Camera-ready.

Elaine asked, "Was the dollhouse a Christmas present?"

"I don't recall." The dollhouse was part of the murky blur that made up too much of her childhood.

"Who would have thought that poor Bob Lindahl was so artistic? He made this with his own hands."

"Everyone has a good side." Rue blinked to erase her most recent memory of Lindahl. Falling to his knees in his driveway. Shot three times in the chest. Dying.

When her stepfather and Cody came into the room, she could tell the two men had been arguing.

An ominous chord sounded inside her head—a portent of more trouble to come.

She avoided looking at Danny. There was no way she could bring herself to deliver the message from the man in the hooded sweatshirt. *Tell Danny to pay and nobody gets hurt.* How could she say that? How could she cast doubt on the successful life he'd created for himself with his new family?

Cody stepped up beside her. "We should be going. Danny has another appointment this afternoon."

The two blond children ran toward him. Both of them singing about Rudolph and his nose so bright.

Once upon a time, that had been Rue. Clinging to Danny and beaming as hard as she could so he would smile back at her. Notice her. Love her.

She forced a smile and said, "I think I should leave the dollhouse here where someone can play with it."

"That's a very sweet gesture," Elaine said. "We'll take good care of it."

The little blond girl left Danny and tugged on Rue's sleeve. "Are you coming to my show? I'm going to be a beautiful angel."

"I should have mentioned it," Elaine said. "Next Sunday evening at St. Jude's the kids are putting on a Christmas program. We'd love to see you, Rue."

"It's already on my schedule," she said. "I'm bringing a Santa Claus cake."

Quickly, she and Cody left the house. She didn't argue when he asked to drive the van. Exhausted, Rue slumped in the passenger seat, staring up at a pristine blue Colorado sky. It didn't seem right for the day to be beautiful when her thoughts were so ugly. Was she some kind of monster? So caught up in her own loneliness that she couldn't stand for anyone else to have a happy life?

Reaching into her purse, she took out the small square box that Elaine had given her.

"What's that?" Cody asked.

"My Christmas present from their family."

She peeled off the crimson wrapping and opened a small white box. Inside was a round silver ornament decorated with a photograph of Danny, his wife and the two adorable blond stepchildren.

She held it up so Cody could see. "What am I going to do with this? I don't have a tree. I can't even go to my house because it's too dangerous for me to be alone."

"You have a home with me," he said.

His smile was gentle and warm. When he reached over and stroked her cheek, some of the ache went away. Right now, he was her haven. "My protector."

He winked. "Somebody's got to watch over you."

And she was grateful. If he hadn't been here, she might have melted into a blubbering mess of forlorn sadness. "How was your talk with Danny?"

"He knows something, but he's not talking."

"Maybe Mike Blanco will tell us what we need to know."

"Tomorrow," he said. "I couldn't set up a meeting with him for today, so tomorrow will have to do."

She was glad. Their conversation with Blanco promised to be filled with even more conflict, and Rue didn't think she could take any more frustration. "What are we going to do for the rest of today?"

"I have plans." His grin widened. "Get ready."

"For what?"

"Tonight, we're going to have ourselves a merry little Christmas."

Chapter Fifteen

Considering that Rue's day had started so badly, it ended very well indeed. It was after ten o'clock. She stood alone in the living room of Cody's seventeenth-floor condo and happily admired the prettiest Christmas tree she'd ever seen—a real tree, Scotch pine and smelling of forests. Strings of multicolored lights twinkled. Popcorn and cranberry garlands draped from the boughs. Among the shiny ornaments were dozens of tinfoil snowflakes, striped candy canes and iced cookies hung by red ribbons.

Though it wasn't December twenty-fifth, this was the best Christmas she'd ever had. Cody had summoned his family to help decorate. Bringing the tree, they arrived in a noisy, boisterous horde. Brothers, sisters, cousins, nieces and nephews.

With her stepfamily history, Rue was accustomed to being surrounded by people she didn't know very well for the holidays. At first, she'd held back—

smiling politely, wondering where these people got their energy and wishing they would leave her alone.

Almost imperceptibly her attitude changed. She was among the Berringers, in their midst instead of being an onlooker.

The difference was Cody. He wrangled his family like a sheepdog with his flock, sending them in all directions with different Christmas chores and bringing them back together. His laughter sparked a chain reaction of cheer.

Their love for Cody—the oldest brother—was a given. Because he cared about her, they did, too. They wanted her there.

Humming "Silver Bells," he came up beside her and placed a mug of hot buttered rum in her hand. "Merry Christmas."

"I love your family."

"I thought they'd never leave."

She still couldn't believe they'd accepted her so quickly. "Are they like that with everyone?"

"You're special."

"Why?"

"Because I said so, and nobody messes with me."

"At the risk of sounding like your three-year-old niece, may I ask why again?"

"Christmas miracle?"

"Why me?"

He groaned. "I suppose you want to hear the whole sad story."

"Yes, please."

He guided her to the sofa and pulled her down beside him. "After my father died, the holidays were tough. Nobody felt like celebrating. Mom was locked up in her room, depressed. My aunts and uncles stayed away, not wanting to intrude on our grief. Nobody knew how to handle us. Happy families aren't supposed to break apart."

His rueful smile hinted at sadness, but Cody lacked his usual cynicism. His story had no ulterior motive; he was sharing a glimpse of his past with her.

"It was up to me," he said. "It was my job as the oldest brother. The so-called man of the family even though I was only twelve. I had to make Christmas happen."

"What did you do?"

"First, I kicked some butt. None of us Berringer kids were going to lie around feeling sorry for ourselves. Everybody got in gear. Decorating. Singing carols. Making gifts for each other. Man, we were moving. Like Santa's elves on speed." He swirled his hot buttered rum. "Alcohol would have been useful, but we were a little young."

"And you've kept up the energy all these years?"

"Not really." His gaze rested on the tree. "This is the first time I've decorated this condo."

And now she understood why his family had responded so quickly and with such enthusiasm. They wanted to pay him back for giving them Christmas so many years ago. Theirs was the sweetest debt—a return of affection and warmth. "Why now? What made you decide to celebrate now?"

"You." He tucked her hair behind her ear. "All your many and varied families were letting you down. You needed some cheer."

Her gaze sank into his. She was seeing him differently than before. Even though they'd been as intimate as a man and a woman could be, theirs wasn't a long-term relationship. No commitments. No demands.

Until now, she hadn't allowed herself to feel deeply. Falling in love was risky, and her heart had been broken too many times. But how else could she feel about a man who protected her, saved her life and gave her a sense of belonging? "You're a good person, Cody Berringer."

"So are you, Ruth Ann Harris."

They slipped into a contented embrace lit by the twinkling star atop the Christmas tree. "I'll never forget this night."

He brushed his lips across her forehead. "It's about time you had some good memories."

"Agreed." Her body molded against him. She wanted to stay in his arms forever.

THE NEXT DAY, Monday, Cody almost canceled their meeting with Mike Blanco. These past few days he'd spent with Rue had given him a different perspective. For twenty years, the quest to find his father's killer had clenched around his heart like a fist. Now the grasp had loosened.

While he'd been making a happy Christmas for Rue, he'd remembered what it felt like to laugh, to love, to embrace his family. His mood was dangerously near happiness.

But finding the murderer was about more than avenging his father. Rue was still in danger. They needed to talk to Mike Blanco.

At two o'clock in the afternoon, they drove through the solidly middle-class neighborhood where Blanco lived. These one-story brick houses had been built after the Second World War when Denver had experienced a population boom. Many of the soldiers who had been stationed at Lowry or hospitalized at Fitzsimmons realized that this city was a good place to settle down. They fell in love with the rugged mountain horizon, the blue skies and sunshine.

Today was just such a perfect Colorado day. The snow had melted. Temperatures hovered in the fifties, warm enough to get by with just a sweater and jeans. Vacation clothes. He'd stopped by his office this morning and delegated his workload. "It doesn't feel like we're investigating a murder."

"That's because *you* haven't had Mel the bodyguard following *you* around all day at the shop."

"He seems unobtrusive," Cody said.

"I can't even walk out to the Dumpster without having him at my heels. He almost tackled a customer who happened to be wearing a hooded sweatshirt." She shrugged. "Not that I'm complaining. I'd rather have Mel than be surprised by the killer."

The bodyguard parked at the curb behind them. As soon as Cody opened his car door, Mel was standing beside him. Gruffly, he said, "I'll accompany you into the house."

"Not necessary."

"This guy is a suspect." Behind his dark glasses, his gaze flicked left and right. "I'm not taking any chances."

Cody didn't argue. He didn't expect this interview with Mike Blanco to be dangerous, but he still hadn't forgotten his mistake yesterday morning when he'd left Rue alone and she'd been confronted by the man in the hooded sweatshirt.

The three of them went up the sidewalk to the doorstep where Mike Blanco answered. With his complexion washed out and his body wasted away, he looked like a pale shadow. His gray, translucent eyes focused on Mel. "A bodyguard?"

Rue introduced them and said, "Danny wants me to be protected."

"He always cared a whole lot about you."

She held out a white cardboard cake box. "This is a low-sugar carrot cake. Not exactly health food, but I hope it's something you can eat."

"Don't you worry," Blanco said. "I'm always looking for food that makes me pack on a few pounds. The docs tell me I need more exercise, but I'm so doggoned pooped that I can hardly drag my butt out of bed in the morning."

It was hard to believe that this guy was the same

age as Danny. No matter what else Cody thought of Rue's stepfather, Danny was robust, aggressively healthy and in his prime—taking on the demanding job of mayor and being stepfather to young children. Mike Blanco seemed to be twenty years his senior, and his speech patterns were those of a much older man. Life had been hard on Blanco. The interior of his house was dimly lit and depressing with worn furniture, clutter on the tables and the stale smell of old man. No Christmas decorations here. A television talk show chattered mindlessly in the background.

Blanco planted himself in the easy chair that was obviously his favorite place. "I don't get many visitors."

No kidding. It might help if he opened a window and aired the place out. Sitting on the sofa beside Rue, Cody listened while she gently inquired about Blanco's health and hobbies. With his apparent physical weakness and folksy manner, the old man didn't seem like much of a threat.

Cody didn't yet have a read on him. "Mind if I ask you a few questions?"

"Sure thing. What can I do you for?"

"I assume you know about the murder weapon that killed Bob Lindahl."

"Sure as heck do. It was the same gun that killed your daddy."

"I don't believe it's a coincidence," Cody said.

"And you want to find out if I know anything." His eyes narrowed as if he were shrewdly calculating how much he should say. "I can tell you this much, your daddy had a lot of folks ticked off."

"The police scandal," Cody said. "What can you tell me about that?"

"Lucky Ted was on the right track. The punks in those gangs made a lot of dough. Drug money. Dirty money. It took some gumption to look the other way when somebody held out a bribe."

From his research, Cody knew that Blanco had been investigated and cleared. "But you were clean."

"Do I look like somebody who made a lot of extra cash?" He gestured weakly to the pathetic furnishings of his house. "This is the reward you get for being an honest cop and playing by the rules."

"Which is what you did."

"Heck, yes. Are you accusing me?"

"Of course not," Rue said. Her gentle voice calmed the waters. "You stayed on the force. You're a respected retiree."

"And it didn't get me very far. I deserve a whole lot more than this."

"Like the kind of money Lindahl made," Cody said. "Did you ever wonder about him? If he was on the take?"

"Whoa there. Even if I knew something—and I'm not saying that I did—I wouldn't rat on my friends."

"But Lindahl is dead," Cody pointed out. "Nothing you say can hurt him now. You must have wondered where your good friend got all the upfront capital he needed to start his construction company. Building those houses cost a lot of money."

"A pretty penny."

Cody's research had already shown that Lindahl's finances were mostly clean, but Blanco didn't know that. "Maybe Lindahl didn't actually take cash but traded favors with criminals. His success came fast."

"And he got too doggoned big for his britches," Blanco said. "All of a sudden, he was too important to be hanging around with the likes of me. A regular hotshot. Know what I mean?"

Cody nodded, encouraging him to continue. "I know."

"And that goes double for Mr. Danny Mason, our new mayor. Sorry, Rue. But Danny couldn't wait to dump his old friends and move into the big time."

She protested, "He stayed close to a lot of people."

"But not me," Blanco said angrily. "Him and me and Lindahl were the three amigos. We did everything together until the two of them moved into their big fancy houses and started drinking champagne instead of good, old, honest beer."

Clearly, he resented the success of his two former friends. It occurred to Cody that Blanco might have been the person who'd sent him the anonymous package with the shamrock tiepin and the bumper sticker with Danny's name. Making trouble for Danny would satisfy some of his bitterness.

"You wanted to get even," Cody said.

His lips curled in an ugly smirk. "The other two amigos weren't as smart as they thought."

"Were they dumb enough to take bribes?" Cody asked. "It's important for me to know. Your information is valuable to me."

"Valuable, huh?"

His eyes brightened, and he sat up a bit straighter in his easy chair. Blanco had an avaricious streak, and Cody played to his greed by saying, "I'd pay for verifiable information. Something I could use."

"I know you've got the money."

"You help me, and I'll help you."

Cody sat back and waited for the proposition. Blanco was the type who thought he deserved more than he was worth. He blamed others for his shortcomings and his bad luck. His attitude was typical of a blackmailer.

If he had evidence that Lindahl and Danny were taking bribes, he might have used that information to extract favors from both of them. And if he had evidence pertaining to the murder of Cody's father?

Rue nudged her thigh against his, and Cody leaned back to look in her direction. Switching his focus to her was a good tactic; it showed he was cool and calm in this negotiation. It also pleased him to look at her. Her chin tilted as if she wanted to ask a question, but she followed his lead and stayed quiet. Waiting.

The creases on Blanco's forehead deepened. He

seemed to be concentrating. Not an intelligent man but sly. Sneaky. He cleared his throat. "I could sure use a new car. My old truck is on her last legs."

A new vehicle was a steep price. Either Blanco had killer proof or he was delusional.

Calmly, Cody said, "My brother is a mechanic. He has contacts with all the car dealers in town."

"My son could use a new car, too."

Why had he mentioned his son? In their earlier contact, he lied to Rue about his son being back east with his mother. "Are you close to your son?"

"Close enough."

Rue spoke up, "You said he lives with his mother but might be visiting you for Christmas."

"Yessiree, you got that right."

If he was lying about something as unimportant as his son's location, his other information might also be false. "Come on now," Cody said, "your boy is in school at Fort Collins."

"That's just plain wrong." His face went even more pale. "He's nowhere near here."

"I looked up his address," Cody said.

"You shouldn't have done that. You've got no right to be prying into my personal affairs."

Cody lowered his hands in a calming gesture. "You're right. It's none of my business where your son lives. Let's get back to—"

"I got nothing more to say." The old man wobbled to his feet. "I'll thank you to leave."

With the glimmer of information fading into

darkness, Cody didn't bother with being subtle. "You know something about my father's murder."

"Nothing I'm going to tell you."

"Was it you? Did you send me the anonymous package with the tiepin and the bumper sticker from Danny's campaign?"

"Get out."

He flapped his hands, trying to shoo them out the door. Cody didn't budge; he wouldn't get another chance with this man and he had to make these moments count. "Here's what I think happened. You blackmailed Danny and Lindahl."

"Does this dump look like I've been raking in the big bucks with a blackmail scheme?"

Cody didn't see Blanco as the kind of person who spent money on showy objects. More than likely, he'd take his blackmail in cash and hide it under a floorboard. "You can tell me."

"And go to jail? I don't want to die in jail."

"I'll take care of you," Cody promised. "You can tell me the truth. Did you arrange with your old amigo buddies to pay for your silence?"

"My silence?" Blanco's narrow shoulders shuddered. "Who the hell is going to listen to a sick, tired, old man like me? My silence ain't worth a plugged nickel."

He was right. To pull off a successful blackmail scam, he needed tangible evidence. A photograph. Or a written document. Or… "The gun. You had the murder weapon all these years. You used it to black-mail Danny or Lindahl or both of them."

When Blanco didn't deny it, Cody continued, "But they got tired of paying. And you shot Lindahl using the same murder weapon."

Instead of crumbling under the weight of Cody's logic, the old man cackled. "Then I must be the doggoned dumbest blackmailer in the whole wide world. If I'd done like you said, I gave away my evidence."

He was right. Cody's assumptions collapsed in a heap.

Chapter Sixteen

As they drove away from Blanco's dismal little house, Rue's mind raced through all the issues that had been raised.

First, there was the possible blackmail scam focused on Danny and Lindahl. But what had they done? The range of possibilities went from taking a few minor bribes to murdering Cody's father—a possibility she simply refused to accept. Danny wasn't a murderer.

Then, there was the craziness about Blanco's son. Why did he keep lying about where his son lived? What was the big deal about an address?

And what else? She remembered that Cody had mentioned something about an anonymous package and a bumper sticker. What was that about?

Her thoughts were as jumbled as lettuce in a salad spinner. She glanced toward Cody. "Are you as confused as I am?"

"That depends. How confused are you?"

"Nothing adds up. If Blanco is a blackmailer, what did he do with the money? He certainly didn't spend it on his house or clothes, and he says he needs a new car."

"Blackmail isn't always about the money."

"Then what? Power?"

Cody nodded. "Mike Blanco is the kind of guy who'd enjoy jerking somebody else's strings, having a secret to hold over his friends."

"Like a troll," she said. "A nasty, evil troll who keeps his precious secrets locked up."

"Interesting comparison," Cody said sardonically. "I didn't know that you were into fairy tales."

"Let's just say that I've known a few trolls, and I think you're right about Blanco." Easily, she imagined the gaunt, white-haired man creeping around his dingy house and cackling about his cleverness. "He's one of those guys who's going to die alone and apparently penniless. Then, someday, they'll discover that he stuffed his mattress with hundred-dollar bills. No wonder he never remarried. I'm kind of amazed that he found *anyone* who would live with him."

Cody turned north on Logan Street, headed back toward downtown. "For somebody who tries to see the good in others, you sound disgusted. Not willing to cut that sick old man some slack?"

"I hate selfishness."

"I guess so."

She indulged herself with a quick study of his rugged features. His firm lips. His amazing azure eyes. If this was a fairy tale, he would be cast as the handsome prince who was courageous, loyal and wise. "Your lack of selfishness might be the reason I was attracted to you from the very start."

"Me? The corporate shark?"

"The first time I saw you was in a Santa Claus suit. Who could be more giving?"

If anything, his subsequent behavior had been even more chivalrous. He'd put his own life on hold to protect her, to give her the happiness of a family Christmas. His generosity was more important to her than his wealth, his success or his totally gorgeous body. She was falling in love with the essential man inside the handsome exterior package...not that she'd throw away the wrapping.

Dragging her gaze away from him, she returned to another puzzling question that had been raised in their conversation with Blanco. "I wonder how his son felt about having a troll for a father."

"The son," Cody said, "is the key to understanding Blanco. You saw how agitated he got when I mentioned his kid."

She nodded. "He was ready to throw us out."

"What if the old man passed the blackmail money on to his son? That would explain why he doesn't want us to find him."

"That's brilliant. We need to talk to Blanco's son."

"I've tried to make contact. His roommates in Fort Collins say they haven't seen him in a couple of weeks."

"Then our next investigative job is to track him down."

"Not us," he said. "I have a private investigator on my payroll. He can take care of locating Blanco's son."

Everything seemed to be falling neatly into place, but she had one more question. "You mentioned something about an anonymous package. Something Blanco might have sent to you?"

"I did."

Cody seemed preoccupied with something he saw in the rearview mirror. She turned in her seat to look over her shoulder. "Is there something behind us?"

"Another car got between us and Mel."

"Somebody following us?"

"Could be."

She remembered the first time she'd been in the passenger seat of his Mercedes, and he'd hinted at how he might enjoy a high-speed chase. *Not her idea of a good time.*

Digging into her purse, she pulled out her cell phone and punched the speed-dial number for Mel. He answered right away.

Rue didn't waste time. "Do you think that other car is tailing us?"

"Tell Cody to take a left at the next corner, then another left on Broadway. If the other car follows, we've got a problem."

She passed on the information and braced herself as Cody whipped a quick left. Then another. This section of Broadway was four lanes headed south. Though it was midafternoon, the traffic between stoplights was heavy.

Mel spoke through the cell phone. "He's still on your tail. Speed up."

"It's not possible," she said. "There are too many other cars."

And Cody had his own plan. "Tell him I'm getting on the highway."

Imagining a wild ride at a hundred and twenty miles per hour, she shook her head. "I don't think so."

Through the cell phone, Mel said, "I heard what he said. The highway is good. It's a go."

"No."

Cody punched the accelerator. In quick spurts, he zipped from one lane to another. Maneuvering like an expert, he found space where none existed. He was good at this. A NASCAR ace. If she hadn't been scared out of her head, she would have complimented him.

Their front bumper barely missed the tail of an SUV. Her muscles tensed as her heel pressed down hard on the floor, wishing for a brake.

"Is he still behind us?" Cody asked.

She scanned through the back window. "One lane over. Two cars back."

"And Mel?"

"I think we've lost him." She held up the cell phone. "Where are you, Mel?"

"I can see you."

The car that had been following eased up behind them again. What was he going to do? Shoot out the back window? Why was he after them?

Then she saw the red and blue flashers from a light that had been attached to the roof. A cop car! "An unmarked cop car. Pull over."

"Son of a bitch," Cody muttered as he eased into the parking lot outside a gas station. As soon as he threw the Mercedes into Park, he was out of the car and charging toward the police vehicle.

Rue was right behind him. Her tension transformed to anger. The police shouldn't be following them; they should be looking for the killer.

Detective Aaron Abbott emerged from the driver's side and faced them.

Cody spoke first. "Why the hell are you following us?"

"I could give you a ticket for the way you were driving. Speeding. Making illegal lane changes."

"Cite me," Cody challenged. "But answer my question first."

"I don't have to justify my actions. I don't answer to you."

Rue inserted herself between the two men. "Detective Abbot, I think we deserve to know why you were following us."

"Doing my job," he snapped.

"Does that mean you've reopened the investigation? That you're still looking for the man who killed Lindahl?"

"This is still an active investigation." He glared at her. "Even though I'm sure we've got the killer. It's Madigan."

"But he was in jail when Tyler Zubek was murdered."

Abbott winced. He had to know that his case against Madigan was flawed; only a complete moron would believe that the two murders were unrelated. "I know."

She kept her voice calm. "Do you have any leads on Tyler's murder? Is there anything that—"

"Back off." His gaze encompassed both of them. "There's nothing else you can do. Leave the investigating to the police."

Rue had heard those words before. "Danny told you to follow us, didn't he?"

"I don't take my orders from—"

"The hell you don't," Cody interrupted. "He's the mayor."

Though Rue was furious, she tried to find something good about this situation—something that would turn lemons into lemonade. "Cody and I have found leads you might want to follow in your investigation. I'll leave him to explain."

She turned on her heel and went back to the Mercedes, slamming the door as she sank into the passenger seat. She hated the way Danny was interfering in her life. Sending the police to follow her. Hiring a bodyguard. Telling her, again and again, to quit investigating. Was it because he cared about her well-being? Or was there another reason?

When she was a kid, Danny was her world—a big, strong father figure who coached her team, taught her how to throw a baseball, took her along on errands and told her bedtime stories. She hated to lose that image, but her admiration for Danny was fading fast.

Obviously, he knew how to play the political game. He'd gone from being a cop to owning a shared interest in several businesses. Much of his success was based on exchanging favors. He was a manipulator.

She knew this firsthand; she went to college on a scholarship from one of Danny's buddies. Yes, she had the grades and the necessary qualifications, but she might not have gotten the scholarship without Danny's recommendation.

When Danny was on your side, everything flowed smoothly. And when he was not? What else had he manipulated?

She thought of Carlos—the witness who had picked Madigan out of the lineup. Danny had plenty of influence with him. He'd hired Carlos to work for him.

And Tyler? Did he agree at first to name Madigan and then change his mind? She didn't want to believe that Danny had had Tyler killed, but that was the message from the man in the hooded sweatshirt.

This can't be. She blocked her suspicions and her memories. She couldn't accuse Danny.

Cody slid behind the passenger seat. The tenderness in his gaze cut through her like a knife. She hadn't been completely honest with him, hadn't told him about the accusation from the man in the hooded sweatshirt.

"Abbott's an okay guy," he said. "He intends to question Mike Blanco and put out an APB on his son."

"Great." But she wasn't feeling great. Her loyalties twisted in a knot. How could she suspect Danny? How could she not tell Cody about those suspicions?

"There's something else I need to explain," he said. "You mentioned the anonymous package."

She'd almost forgotten. "With a bumper sticker?"

"A bumper sticker from Danny's campaign and a gold shamrock tiepin, similar to one my father used to wear. Actually, he had several. The shamrock tiepin was his Lucky Ted trademark."

"A four-leaf clover. A symbol of luck."

He took her hand, and his warmth flowed through her. "Somebody sent me that package a week before Lindahl's party for Danny."

"And you think it was Blanco? Why?"

"He's a conniving man. What did you call him? A troll. He might have wanted to stir things up and cause trouble for Danny. When I first got the package, I considered going to the police and demanding that they reopen their investigation into my father's murder."

"A cold case," she said.

"Ice-cold. That's why I decided not to bother with regular channels. I could investigate myself, and the message was obvious: Danny—the new mayor of Denver—was connected to my father's death."

Unfortunately, his deduction made perfect sense to her. Every new detail they uncovered seemed to point directly at Danny. "Why didn't you mention the package before?"

"Two reasons," he said. "The first is that you don't take kindly to accusations against your former stepfather."

A possibly misplaced loyalty that was rapidly changing to mistrust. "And the second?"

"That anonymous package was the reason I asked you out. You seemed like a person who could help me get close to Danny."

She already knew about his initial reasons for wanting to be with her, and she'd made her peace with it. "We've been over this before. You were using me."

"I just want you to know," he said as he turned the key in the ignition and listened to the smooth hum of the Mercedes's engine. "I'm not that guy anymore."

Chapter Seventeen

Much to Cody's frustration, the next several days passed without their investigation moving forward. Mel was a constant but unobstrusive presence, but they had no further contact from the man in the hooded sweatshirt. Detective Abbott had contacted him a couple times to inform him that the police were unable to locate Blanco's son.

On Thursday, he and Rue returned to her duplex so she could pick up more clothing and water the plants. Her cute little home had taken on an empty feel in her absence.

She traced her finger through the accumulated dust on the bookshelf. "I could probably move back here. Things seem to have settled down."

"Forget it," he said quickly. "This place is an invitation to a break-in."

"It's not that bad."

"If you don't mind living in a glass house. Look at all these windows. You've got no protection here.".

Her eyes shone with a soft, welcoming light as she came closer to him and reached up to stroke his cheek. "Staying at your place makes me feel like I'm taking advantage of you."

"I like having you around," he said. "You're good for me. I'm eating more healthy food now than I ever have in my life."

"Like I'm your personal chef?" she teased.

My personal everything. "You're staying with me."

On the tip of his tongue was a proposal to make that arrangement permanent. But making that kind of commitment ran contrary to his personal code. At least, that was the way he used to think. Now he wasn't so sure.

In spite of his best efforts to be a workaholic attorney who kicked butt in negotiations and won every argument, he was turning into someone who was a lot more like his father. Altruistic. Making time for his family. Taking off work. Laughing. And making love.

Especially making love. The hours they spent in bed together got better and better. She seemed more beautiful to him every day.

On Friday, Rue came with him to the mall to help shop for family Christmas presents. Though she'd only met the whole Berringer mob once, she was better able than he to point out the right gift for the right person.

Near the cosmetics counter, she held up a tube of liquid. "Heavy-duty hand cream for your sister."

"Why?"

"Because she loves gardening which is hard on the hands, and this is within the ten-dollar limit that your family puts on gifts."

"Thoughtful," he said. His usual procedure was to buy gift certificates for everybody. Some years, he didn't even make that effort. He'd send his secretary out to make the purchases and stuff them into his standard Christmas card with the engraved signature.

Being with Rue made shopping kind of enjoyable—jostling through the crowds, picking and choosing. It wasn't much fun for Mel who was constantly scanning the crowd.

At the line of children and parents waiting to sit on Santa's lap, she came to a halt. "I'm going to leave you here for a couple of minutes and go off with Mel."

He arched an eyebrow. "Was it something I said?"

"I need to find your present," she said. "Be right back."

Abandoned by Rue, he realized that he needed to find a present for her. Something special. Something that would tell her how important she was to him. His gaze scanned the shops. Chocolates? Calendars? Shoes? Jewelry!

He went directly to the diamond counter and looked down at the glittering display. A necklace? Earrings? Bracelets? A ring!

An engagement ring. Without considering the meaning of this gift, he asked the clerk to show him an array. It wasn't the largest stone that caught his eye but a flawless yellow diamond set between an emerald and a sapphire that reminded him of the blue-green-hazel of her eyes. This ring was perfect for Rue. He made the purchase and slipped the small velvet box into his pocket.

He couldn't believe that he was thinking of marriage and settling down. Hell, nobody would believe it. Especially not Rue. He hadn't even told her that he loved her.

Instead of the panic he expected to feel at such a time, he realized that he was smiling. His heart swelled. This was good. This was the right thing to do.

ON SATURDAY, Rue was in her shop, putting the last flourishes on the cakes she'd promised for the church Christmas party where Danny's young stepchildren would be singing carols. Though she hadn't spoken to Danny since last Sunday when they stopped by his house, he'd popped into her thoughts frequently… and not in a good way.

Her happy memories of Danny had turned sour. She had too many suspicions about why Blanco might be blackmailing him.

Bernice breezed into the kitchen. During the countdown to Christmas, she'd taken to decorating her poufy blond hair with sprigs of mistletoe—an unsubtle invitation to a kiss.

"Love the cakes," she said.

Both were round, frosted in white, with Santa's face in the middle. "When I get to the church, I'll add a couple of poinsettias."

Bernice perched on a high stool and crossed her long legs. "What's your Christmas present for Cody?"

"I gathered up a bunch of family photos from his house, and I'm having them framed." She wasn't totally comfortable with her choice of present. "Is that too pushy? It's like I'm redecorating his home."

"If he doesn't like it, he won't hesitate to tell you. Tact isn't his best attribute."

"But he has so many others." Rue flashed on a memory of this morning when she'd watched him shaving. He'd stood at the bathroom mirror wearing only a towel. She'd crept up behind him and stretched her hands across the span of his broad shoulders, massaged his sculpted shoulder blades and his lean torso. Exhaling a wistful sigh, she said, "Many, many attributes."

"Tell," Bernice said.

"Not a chance."

"Being with Cody has done wonders for your complexion, sweetie. You're glowing."

Instead of making a self-deprecatory comment about the red glow of Rudolph's nose, she simply said, "Thank you."

Leticia whipped through the rear door of the shop, stomped her Gucci boots on the mat and brushed a few flakes of snow off her shoulder. "So glad I caught you in, Rue. I've been meaning to get over here for days."

"Hi, Mom."

"Are you going to the Christmas party at St. Jude's Episcopal?"

Rue gestured to the cake. "I'm providing the refreshments."

"The judge and I have another commitment so I won't be able to make it, even though I was on the committee that raised money to repair the carillon bells. You know they're going to ring for the first time in ten years. At eight o'clock tonight."

"I know."

"It seemed to me that they should wait until New Year's Eve, but I suppose this is just as well."

Leticia shed her coat, exchanged air kisses with Bernice and waved for them both to come into the office. "I found pictures."

Like Cody, Leticia kept her family photos tucked away. Somewhere between the third and fourth husband, she'd told Rue that it was too complicated to figure out who should go on the wall. Rather than insult any of her former spouses or step-relations, she'd gone with a Chinese wall hanging.

From a manila folder, Leticia produced a series of informal snapshots. "The dollhouse that Bob Lindahl made for you is in every one of these photos."

Bernice picked up a snapshot of Rue in her Little League uniform. "Oh my God, you were adorable."

"She was," Leticia agreed. "A little tomboy with skinned knees and a smudge of dirt on her nose."

"And the long braids," Bernice said.

"Every morning, I'd braid her hair." Rue's mother smiled fondly. "That was our time together."

The fondness in Leticia's voice struck a chord

with Rue. No matter how crazy and disrupted her childhood had been, her mother had been there for her. While Rue was busy trying to find her father figure, her mother waited and watched and made sure her hair was carefully braided.

She hugged her mother's slender shoulders. "Thank you for hanging in there with me."

"You've always been a wonderful daughter. Perhaps I haven't told you often enough?"

"You were a great mom." She glanced at Bernice. "She was always the prettiest mom in the whole class."

"I suppose that counts for something."

"It counts," Rue assured her. "Are you sure that you and the judge won't be able to join me at the Berringers' for Christmas Day?"

"We were planning to be at the condo in Vail, but we might make it down. We'll try."

Bernice held up another photo. "Who's the boy in this picture?"

"Jerome Samuels." Rue studied the snapshot. She and Jerome were standing beside the dollhouse. He'd crossed his arms on his skinny chest and scowled, trying to look tough. It wasn't an act; Jerome had been in a gang. "When Danny started his negotiations with the gangs, Jerome was over at our house a lot."

"A nice-looking boy," Leticia said. "And very polite. He must have been thirteen in this picture."

"I was almost six."

"And it's summertime," Leticia said. "This photo

proves that I was wrong about when you got the doll-house. It wasn't a Christmas present."

"I knew it," Rue said.

A doorway to very old memories cracked open. In the back of her mind, she heard Uncle Bob saying that her gift was too late for the previous Christmas and too early for the next one. But he wanted her to have it. The first house he'd ever built.

Mike Blanco had been there, too. Twenty years ago, he'd been dark-haired and kind of handsome—nothing like the troll he'd become.

And Jerome… "The timing is wrong," she said.

"What do you mean?"

"This picture was taken the summer *before* Danny started negotiations with the gangs."

Leticia nodded. "Yes."

"That means Danny knew Jerome *before* the negotiations started. *Before* Lucky Ted Berringer was shot and killed."

"And why is that important?"

Because it meant Danny had contacts inside the gangs prior to starting the negotiations, and he was close to Jerome—a thirteen-year-old boy with a chip on his shoulder.

She remembered being with Jerome. They weren't playing because he was too old to be interested in her kind of games, but they'd throw the baseball back and forth. Or he'd hit long flies, and she'd chase the ball down. Mostly, they hung out. Listening.

Jerome had access to inside information from

Danny and the other two amigos. She stretched her deductions further. If Danny had known about Lucky Ted's meeting with the informant, Jerome would have had the same information. He could have passed it on to someone else in the gang. To the killer.

Possibly, as Cody had suggested, Lucky Ted planned to be accompanied by a cop at his warehouse meeting. A cop like Danny?

She turned toward her mother. "On the night when Lucky Ted was killed, where was Danny?"

"Most of that night, he was home with me. The only time he went out was when he picked you up from a friend's house. It was late. Around ten o'clock. And you stopped at a convenience store to pick up milk."

"He was with me?"

"Yes, dear."

The irony of that information took a moment to sink in. Danny couldn't have killed Cody's father.

Rue was his alibi.

WAITING FOR Rue at his condo, Cody sat on the sofa facing the Christmas tree. In the palm of his hand, he held the velvet box with the diamond ring—a symbol of love eternal. He imagined being married to Rue. They'd live in the condo for a few years, but then they'd need a house. For their children. Not a big family. Just two kids. A boy and a girl with long, wavy hair like Rue.

For most of his life, he'd been looking backwards, focused on his father's murder. Now he reveled in the possibilities of the future. He wanted to get started, to give her the ring now. This minute.

He heard Rue crash through the door and quickly slipped the ring into his suit coat pocket. Maybe not right now.

She raced across the room, clearly excited. Crystals of unmelted snow sparkled in her hair. Her cheeks were rosy. She spread her arms wide and announced, "It was Jerome."

"What about him?"

She dropped a photograph onto his lap. "This picture is proof that Jerome knew Danny before the gang negotiations started. He was in our house, hanging around with cops. He could have known about your father's meeting with the informant."

"Which doesn't necessarily make him the killer," Cody pointed out.

"But he could have told somebody in the gangs."

She dove onto the couch beside him and gave him a sweet, happy kiss that quickly turned sexy. The warmth of her body contrasted the snowflakes that clung to her jacket. His hand slipped inside and cupped her breast.

"Later," she whispered. "Later, we'll make love. Right now I have to change clothes for the Christmas party at the church."

"Doesn't start until seven," he murmured. "An hour from now."

"But I have to get there early to put the finishing touches on my cakes."

He followed her into the bedroom they now shared. Stretched out on the bed, he watched as she unselfconsciously slipped out of her work clothes. His gaze rested on the lacy edge of her pink bra and matching bikini panties. The fact that she wasn't trying to be seductive turned him on more than if she'd been doing a striptease.

"Everything makes sense to me," she said. "The reason Danny was being blackmailed was that he had contacts inside the gangs *before* the negotiations started."

Cody forced himself to focus on her words. "If that's true, he was probably on the take."

"Or it might *look* that way. He could be completely innocent." As always, she was quick to provide Danny with an excuse. "Either way, he wouldn't want that information to become public."

"Hell, no," Cody said. Even a twenty-year-old police corruption scandal would tarnish Danny's political career.

She slipped into a soft green sweater that hugged her curves and a pair of gray wool slacks. "I'm pretty sure Jerome will be at the church tonight. Maybe you can talk to him."

"Why not you?"

"Because Jerome still treats me like I'm an annoying kid with pigtails." She grasped his hand to pull him off the bed. "We need to go."

He rose from the bed and slipped his arms around her. After a quick kiss, she straightened his

necktie. Her delicate fingers touched his tiepin.
"What's this?"

"A gold shamrock." Like his father used to wear.
"I'm feeling lucky tonight."

Chapter Eighteen

After Cody helped Rue carry her cakes into the recreation hall at the church, he skirted the edge of the rows of folding chairs, looking for Jerome.

Instead, he spotted Carlos—the former bodyguard for Bob Lindahl who had identified Madigan as the killer. Apparently, his leg injury from being shot was only a flesh wound. Carlos walked with a cane.

Cody approached and shook his hand. After a few comments about the lightly falling snow, Cody said, "Sorry for your bad luck."

"What bad luck?"

"With your employer dead, you're out of a job."

"You'd think so."

Cody assumed it wasn't a stellar recommendation for a bodyguard to lose his job because the person he was guarding had been murdered. "You've found other work?"

"I'm set," Carlos said coolly. "I'm on Danny's team now."

Of course he was. If Lindahl's murder hinged on blackmail, Danny would do anything to keep the real cause quiet. He needed to keep Carlos close.

When Cody saw Jerome, he excused himself and went toward the tall blond man who had risen from the gangs to a position of power in the world. At what price? The murder of Cody's father?

The truth was so close that Cody could taste the sweetness of revenge on his lips. He faced Jerome. "Once again, we're meeting at a church."

"What do you want, Cody?"

The recreation hall had begun to fill up with parents and friends who would sit in folding chairs to watch the children from Sunday School classes sing carols. At eight o'clock, the program would be followed by the ringing of the bells. Then Santa Claus would show up with a bounty of presents.

Cody glanced at his wristwatch. Only a couple of minutes before the program got underway. No time for small talk. "I need to ask you about the night my father was killed."

"Not again," Jerome said. "You and Rue have got to stop investigating."

"This was twenty years ago. June fourteenth. My father went to a meeting with an informant. And you knew about the time and the place."

A flicker of surprise crossed his face. "Why would you think I had that information?"

"Rue figured out the timing," he said confidently. "You knew."

Jerome looked past Cody's shoulder and shrugged. "We're not having this conversation."

"Fine. I'll pass this on to Detective Abbott. The possibility that you were a witness might be enough to reopen the case. The investigation might be cold but it's not dead. There's no statute of limitations on murder."

The last thing Jerome would want was suspicion. He'd worked his whole life to achieve his current success as the right-hand man of Denver's new mayor. "What do you want from me?"

"Tell me what happened that night."

Jerome's voice was low and angry. "You think your father was some kind of saint, but he was just another attorney. An assistant DA. And he was going to meet with a criminal. To exchange information. To make a deal with the devil."

"That's how the system works." Cody's determination matched Jerome's rage. "You know that."

"The system is wrong. It's not justice."

Cody waited a moment for him to continue. Jerome's complexion darkened. His mouth pinched in a hard line as he struggled to remain silent.

They weren't that different, he and Jerome. They'd both had rough childhoods, both had to deal with tragedies. Cody had lost his father. And Jerome had lost someone, too. "This is about your sister."

"The guy your father was meeting was the shooter in the drive-by that killed my baby sister. And Lucky Ted wanted to let him off the hook. To trade her life for some worthless information about cops on the take."

"He wouldn't have done that," Cody said.

"No? Then why meet with the murderer?"

"How did you know about the meet?"

"I heard somebody talk about it."

"Danny?"

Jerome scoffed at the question. He sure as hell wasn't going to say anything that might implicate the man who was about to give him a new, important job in his administration. "I don't remember."

"What happened that night?" Cody repeated.

Jerome drew himself up straighter. "I wasn't there at the warehouse."

"Who was?"

"I don't know. I wish it had been me. I never would have killed your father, Cody. But that other guy? The snitch?" He exhaled through his nostrils. "I'll tell you the truth. The God's honest truth. I'm glad that snitch is dead."

At the front of the recreation hall the pastor stepped up on the stage in front of a maroon velvet curtain and called everyone to sit. He promised they were in for a real treat.

"I believe you," Cody said.

"I don't give a damn if you believe me or not."

Ironically, that attitude was precisely what convinced Cody that Jerome was innocent of his father's murder. But Danny must have been the person who'd told him. Danny knew about Lucky Ted's meeting at the warehouse. Danny and who else? Maybe Lindahl. Maybe Blanco.

He looked around the hall for Rue. But she was nowhere in sight.

FROM ACROSS the room, Rue had caught a glimpse of Cody. A tall man in a black suit with a gold tiepin. And she knew. A vivid memory assailed her. Something she'd buried for twenty years.

At the back of the reception hall, she leaned against the wall, hidden by shadow. The program had begun.

The clear sound of children's voices singing carols faded to a different tune. A car radio. The soft twang of Willy Nelson's guitar.

It was summer. Twenty years ago. She was almost seven years old. Danny had picked her up from a friend's house, and they were driving home. It was late at night, after ten o'clock, and she was tired. Though she should have been wearing her seat belt, she curled up on the backseat, drowsing.

The night was cool and she was only wearing shorts, so Danny covered her with his patrolman's jacket. It smelled like leather and the man scent that she identified as Danny. Her stepfather. He always took good care of her.

After a while—it could have been a minute or an hour—the car door slammed, and she woke up. Peeking over the front seat through the windshield, she saw Danny walking toward a place they had never been before. The street was scary and full of shadows. Ugly, empty buildings rose up on both sides. No trees.

No people. She wanted to run after Danny, but she was afraid to leave the car.

She kept her eyes trained on Danny. As long as she could see him, she'd be all right. He stood just inside a big open door that was like the front of a garage, and he was talking to somebody she couldn't quite see. A man in a suit.

Danny was angry. She could tell from the way he was standing. The other man stepped into a shaft of light from the streetlamp. He was tall. Black hair. He had a gold pin on his necktie.

Oh my God. Cody.

Standing at the back of the church reception hall, her eyelids squeezed shut. She covered her mouth with both hands to keep from crying out. The man she'd seen with Danny had to be Cody's father. Lucky Ted Berringer.

Carefully, she eased out of the reception hall to the courtyard between the recreation hall and the sanctuary of the church. Snowflakes drifted down, but she didn't feel the cold. Her pulse raced. Her blood surged hotly through her veins. And her memory continued.

Danny had a gun. Light reflected off the silver barrel. *He was a policeman. Sometimes he had to use his gun to fight the bad guys.*

Dozens of times, he'd told her. *Sometimes he had to use his gun…*

She ducked down in the backseat and pulled Danny's jacket over her head, but she still heard the three shots. Pop, pop, pop.

Seconds later, he got back into the car, sat behind the steering wheel.

She kept her eyes closed, pretended to sleep when he turned and tucked his jacket more closely around her. His hands smelled like burnt metal.

He started the engine and the car radio began to play. Deep in her heart, she knew that something wasn't right. She ought to tell somebody. But this was Danny. He wouldn't do the wrong thing.

She must have dreamed the whole thing. Best to forget. Best to keep quiet.

Standing outside the church, she experienced a painful depth of regret. Her need to keep Danny close was more powerful than her memory. Her mind was erased. *It never happened.* She'd never consciously recalled that night. Not until now.

The door from the reception hall opened, and she heard the trailing litany of "a partridge in a pear tree." Cody was walking toward her.

Gently, he folded her into an embrace. "It's cold out here."

"Is it?"

Physically, she felt nothing. All her energy went into suppressing her hopes and dreams for a future with Cody—a beautiful life that could have fulfilled them both.

She remembered Mike Blanco's surprised reaction when he saw them together for the first time. *The son of Lucky Ted and Danny's stepdaughter... Who'd have thunk it?* Blanco had known what would happen between them.

Her past had caught up to her. She'd witnessed the murder and kept silent; Cody could never forgive her.

CODY HELD her as she wept. Violent sobs wracked through her slender body. What the hell brought this on? Who had hurt her so deeply? If it was Danny, if that smug bastard had said something that had torn her apart… "What is it, Rue? You can tell me. I'm right here. What's wrong?"

She lifted her tear-stained face. "How did you find me out here?"

"Mel's doing his job. He pointed me in the right direction."

"Mel!" she shouted his name.

"Right here," came the reply from the shadows.

"Please leave us alone."

"You know I can't—"

"Please! I have to tell Cody something, and I don't want you to hear. Please, Mel. I'm at a church. I couldn't be safer."

"If you need me, I'm right inside."

She waited until she heard the door close. Her breath came in sporadic bursts of vapor. Her fingers were red and raw with the cold as she grasped his lapel. The pain in her eyes cut into his heart.

"I love you, Cody."

"I love you, too." But he hadn't wanted to tell her like this. He had the diamond engagement ring in his pocket. This should have been the happiest moment in both their lives—the moment when the carillon bells would ring out and announce their great joy.

"I wish…" Overwhelmed by a sob, her words halted. She wrenched away from him. "I'd give anything to keep from saying this. But I can't lie to you."

"Saying what?" He felt the cold of the night. With vivid clarity, he saw the sidewalk around the court-yard, dusted with snow. In the center was the snow-covered fountain. Around the edges, the stone sculptures of saints watched from their niches. "What is it, Rue?"

"On the night your father was murdered, I was Danny's alibi. He picked me up from a friend's house at about ten o'clock and took me home."

He waited for her to continue, dreading what came next.

"I was asleep in the back of the car. But I woke up for a moment. And I saw Danny talking to a tall man in a black suit. A man who looked a lot like you do right now—with a gold tiepin. When I saw you standing across the room, I remembered. Before that moment, I had no recollection. Zero. As if it never happened. I swear. I swear in front of all these saints, I didn't remember."

He took a step away from her. Past, present and future collided. There should have been an explosion. Fireworks. But the silence of the night wrapped around them like a shroud. He'd spent most of his life looking for his father's killer. And the answer stood here before him. An eyewitness to the crime.

"Danny had a gun," she said.

"You saw my father die?"

"I ducked down behind the seat. But I heard three shots."

If she'd come forward at the time, she could have saved him a lifetime of misery. "Why didn't you say anything?"

"I was only six."

"Old enough to know right from wrong."

She inhaled a ragged breath. "I must have convinced myself that it was a only dream. I buried the memory. I didn't want to lose Danny."

Instead, she'd lost Cody.

Cody turned on his heel and walked away. He couldn't stand to be with her for one more moment.

Chapter Nineteen

Inside the darkened church, Rue sat alone in the third pew, staring up at the carved cherrywood pulpit. Floral displays of white Christmas lilies and poinsettias lined the box where the choir sat and the edges of the sanctuary below the unlit candles. Moonlight came through the tall arched windows on both sides of the pews and a jewel-toned stained-glass window above the altar. There was a light at the back door and in the sanctuary—just enough to see.

From the recreation hall down two twisting corridors, she heard distant echoes of the Christmas recital—sweet voices singing "Silent Night."

She hadn't come here to pray but to seek solace. Cody had walked away from her, and she didn't blame him for turning his back. Why should he believe that she'd completely erased that terrible night from her memory? She wouldn't have believed herself, except for the other little memories that crawled now from the back of her mind. Ugly memories. Like the time

Danny's temper got the best of him and he purposely drove over the neighbor kid's bike. Or the way he demanded free soda and cigarettes at the drug store. Or his flirting with a red-haired waitress. The way he'd pat her shoulder and say, "Don't tell your Mom about this."

Under the guise of sharing secrets, he'd turned her into his accomplice. She would have done anything to gain his love. Not that Danny knew the meaning of the word.

Love was about caring, trusting, laughing. Love was how she felt about Cody.

Now that was gone.

She wasn't surprised when she looked up and saw Danny standing between the pews. In the moonlight that spilled through the windows, she saw his anger. The set of his shoulders was menacing, but she didn't care. She'd already lost Cody. Nothing else could be worse.

"I remembered," she said. "The night when Cody's father was killed. You used me as your alibi."

"You're mistaken, Ruth Ann. You were never there."

He sounded completely sure of himself. But she knew better than to believe him. This time, he wouldn't get away with murder.

She rose to her feet. "Liar."

"That's a harsh word."

"It's the truth." She stepped into the center aisle to face him. "I saw you. I was in the back of the car, watching. I heard the gunshots."

"Heard them?"

She hadn't actually witnessed the murder; that would have been a trauma too big to ignore. "I saw you facing Cody's father with a gun in your hand."

"I didn't kill him." He came toward her. He was light on his feet, like a boxer. Grasping her arms above the elbows, he gave her a shake. "You've got to believe me."

She'd always thought Danny was a handsome man, with his dark-red hair and laughing eyes. Now she saw a monster—a devil in the sanctuary. "Let go of me. I know what I saw."

"I can explain."

"Let go," she repeated.

He released her and stepped back. "You're right. I was there. That makes me an accessory to murder, but Mike Blanco pulled the trigger. All three of us were there. Me and Bob Lindahl and Blanco. We had to keep Lucky Ted from talking to the snitch."

"And giving evidence about police corruption," she said. "About the bribes you took."

"Not me. Not much anyway." He shrugged. "We were there to tell our side of the story. But Blanco went crazy. He took the gun from my hand. He was supposed to get rid of the weapon. But he hung on to my gun. All these years."

"And hired someone to use it on Lindahl," she said.

"That's right."

His voice was hopeful, encouraging her to believe

him. But she was done with being gullible. "Are you really going to blame everything on that sick old man?"

"It's the truth," Danny protested.

"When did Blanco start blackmailing you?"

He cringed, but when he spoke, his voice was level and calm. "About ten years ago, after Lindahl and I got successful, Blanco started demanding money to keep quiet. It wasn't much. Nickels and dimes. Nothing I couldn't afford. But when I got elected mayor, he wanted more. A hundred thousand dollars."

"And you turned him down."

"I talked it over with Lindahl, and we decided to put on the brakes. That's when Blanco took his revenge. He got somebody to kill Lindahl and leave the gun behind."

She remembered the conversation she and Cody'd had with Blanco, remembered his blackmailer's logic. "Why leave the gun behind? That murder weapon was his only evidence. Without it, you don't have to pay."

"This time, his message was different," Danny said darkly. "This time, it wasn't about money."

"Then what?"

"If Blanco was crazy enough to kill Lindahl, he could come after me. Or my wife. Or you, Ruth Ann."

Her breath caught in her throat. That was why Danny hired Mel to be her bodyguard. "Blanco was using my life to blackmail you."

"Don't worry, Ruth Ann. I paid the hundred thousand." He gave her his utterly false politician's smile. "You're safe now. We're all safe. Everything is going to be all right."

His phony reassurance filled her with revulsion. The inside of her mouth tasted foul. Her stomach churned, and she felt as though she might vomit.

"What about Madigan?" She named the man who was in custody, charged with Lindahl's murder. "The police expect him to talk in exchange for a deal."

Danny gave a casual shrug. "Madigan's got nothing to say. He's not the guy Blanco hired."

"I knew it." She hadn't been able to pick him out of the lineup because he wasn't the killer. "You convinced the other two witnesses—Tyler and Carlos—to lie for you. Did you pay them?"

"Yes."

"Then Tyler wanted more money, and you killed him, too."

"Hell, no. The last thing I wanted was another murder."

She found that hard to believe. He seemed to be extremely comfortable with his life of crime. Murder. Accessory to murder. Taking bribes. Being part of a cover-up.

"And you're all right with Madigan being accused? With letting an innocent man go to jail?"

"Trust me on this. Madigan is a career criminal. He's killed before and deserves to be behind bars."

"So do you."

"You don't mean that." He approached her again. "Come on, Ruth Ann. Don't you remember all the good times we had together? You were my little girl. I was so proud of you."

She would have wept, but her eyes were dry. She'd spent all her tears.

CODY STOOD silently in the shadows behind the pulpit. Watching. Listening. Waiting.

He'd come back to be with Rue. Though he wasn't sure he could ever forgive her for hiding the truth, he could understand how a six-year-old child might not know the right thing to do, especially when her step-father had been pulling the strings—manipulating her like a puppet. *The bastard.*

He understood about suppressed memories. Rue hadn't meant to be secretive. The important thing was what she would do now. Now the truth was out.

He listened carefully to every word Danny spoke. Now Cody was another witness. When these accusations came to trial, he could back up Rue's testimony. *If it came to trial.* He wasn't sure that Rue could force herself to be the instrument of Danny's undoing. Her loyalty blinded her.

Cody was glad that he'd come back. He was ready to help if she needed him. Ready to walk away if she agreed to maintain her twenty-year silence.

RUE LISTENED to the burst of applause from the re-creation hall. The caroling program must be over. The parents and children would be eating her three-layer cakes with cream-cheese frosting. They'd be laughing and hugging. Happy families united in the spirit of Christmas.

In the darkened church, she faced the only man she'd ever thought of as her father. He had been her hero, the man she looked up to and measured all other men against. No one lived up to her idealized version of Danny Mason. Except for Cody.

He was a real hero. From the first time she'd met him, she'd known he wasn't perfect. He'd freely admitted that he'd used her to further his own goals. All he cared about was his obsession with finding his father's killer. And his work. He tried to be a shark who gleefully devoured his opposition. But he couldn't hide his true nature.

Inside—where it really counted—he was a good man. Generous and caring. He loved his family. And her. He loved her.

She owed a debt of honesty to Cody. And to herself. For twenty years, this trauma had been festering inside her. It was time to lance the boil.

She confronted Danny. "I'm going to the police."

"You can't do this to me, Ruth Ann. Think of my family. If you ever loved me, if you ever cared about me at all—"

"Stop it," she snapped. If he had ever cared about her, he would know that she had to do the right thing. "I'm not your alibi. Not anymore."

He drew himself up. "No one will believe you. I'm the mayor. I deserve respect."

"I'm sure you'll get what you deserve."

From the rear of the church, she heard another sound. Someone else approaching. The wheezing cackle identified Mike Blanco before he spoke. "Much as I'd like to see Danny behind bars," he said, "I can't let you go to the cops."

Blanco wasn't alone. Beside him was a man in a hooded sweatshirt. The killer.

They stopped halfway down the center aisle. When the killer swept his hood back, Rue could see the resemblance to the young Mike Blanco she'd seen in photographs. "You're his son. Roger Blanco."

"Clever deduction, Missy. This is my boy."

With that simple introduction, the blackmail scheme made sense to her. Blanco had never wanted the money for himself, not for his own miserable life. He was financing his son, denying that Roger even knew him, trying to hide their connection by saying he lived with his mother.

Somewhere along the line, father and son got together. And the father's hatred turned the son into a killer.

Danny stood beside her. "You've got your money, Blanco. This is none of your business."

"Well now, Mister Mayor, it ain't going to do me and Roger much good to be the richest jailbirds in town."

He should have thought of that before he started killing people. She stared through the dim light at Roger. The man in the hooded sweatshirt who confronted her at the bakery. "You told me that you didn't kill Tyler Zubek."

"Had to happen," his father said. "Young Tyler was threatening to overturn the apple cart."

"I'm not talking to you." She kept her focus on the younger man. A shaft of moonlight illuminated Roger's face. "You lied to me."

"I guess so."

"Why?"

When he grinned, he looked so terribly young. Only a sophomore in college. He should have had his whole life in front of him. "A man's got to do what a man's got to do."

Then she saw the gun in his hand.

She could have pleaded for her life, could have promised that she wouldn't go to the police. But they wouldn't believe her.

Rue was as good as dead.

But she wouldn't give up without a fight.

The carillon bells started ringing. A clamorous pealing split the air.

Rue dodged to her left. Bent double, she raced between the pews. Danny was right behind her. She didn't know whose side he was on. Was he trying to protect her? Or to kill her?

She couldn't distinguish the sound of gunfire from the crashing bells. But she knew Blanco's son was shooting.

Danny cried out. "I'm hit."

She couldn't stop to help him. Had to save herself.

Seeking cover, she climbed over the rail in front of the altar. Ducked behind the pulpit. Trying to avoid the Christmas lilies, she stumbled.

When she regained her feet, she was facing Roger Blanco.

With both arms braced in front of him, he aimed at her face. It was over. Her life was over.

Another figure moved through the shadows. Cody! With a flying tackle, he took Roger down. Neatly, he disarmed him.

Gun in hand, Cody faced the elder Blanco.

The bells had stopped pealing. From the recreation hall, she heard the children squealing in joy at the arrival of Santa Claus.

Cody called out, "Blanco, throw down your weapon."

"Ain't got one." Coughing and wheezing, he was barely able to speak. Clutching his chest, he sank to his knees beside the pews. "My heart. I need an ambulance."

Cody's voice thundered. "You killed my father."

"My heart…" He was gasping. "Help me."

"I want to hear it from your lips."

"Damn you, Cody Berringer. Yes. I killed him."

Cody took his cell phone from his pocket and punched in 911.

Where was Danny?

Rue scrambled back to the end of the pews. Beneath the tall, arched window, Danny sat on the floor, holding his midsection. His blood stained the floor and the wall. The front of his shirt was completely red. How many times had he been shot?

She sank to her knees beside him. Gently, she touched his cheek. "I'm sorry."

"Not your fault, Ruth Ann."

"You're going to be all right," she said desperately. Danny was strong and tough. "You're going to pull through."

"I'm dying." He clutched her hand with a tight grip. "It's better this way. Can't be mayor from jail."

She didn't want him to die. No matter what he had done. "Stay with me, Danny."

His wavering gaze met hers. "I remember when you made that throw from third base to first. A double play." He coughed. "My little girl."

He shuddered and his grasp loosened.

She could feel him slipping away.

Epilogue

After Danny's death, Rue had wanted to be alone with her grief. She left Cody's condo and moved back into her duplex. For once in her life, she was going to feel every emotion. There would be no pushing aside of unpleasant memories, no matter how painful.

She gave her statement to Detective Abbot, but refused to talk to the media. They needed no help in smearing Danny's memory, digging up all the dirt. He hadn't been all bad. Or all good. He was flawed. And there was much about him that she loved.

On Christmas morning, her shop was closed, and she slept late. Until almost nine o'clock.

The phone rang, but she didn't pick up. She heard Cody's deep voice. "Merry Christmas, Rue."

She lay in her bed, not picking up the phone, and whispered, "Merry Christmas, Rue."

It had been eight days since she'd seen him, and his absence tore her apart inside. He was the love of her life. The man she was meant to be with. But too much stood between them.

Over the phone, he said, "Open your front door."

Wrapping herself in a robe and sticking her feet into fuzzy slippers, she went through her house to the door. On the porch was a copy of the morning newspaper with the editorial section on top.

She looked up and down her street, but didn't see Cody anywhere. *What was this all about?*

Carrying the paper inside, she set the coffee to perk and sat down with the paper. There was a long article, written by Cody Berringer. He recounted the story she'd told him about Danny at the gym, winning the right to negotiate with the gangs in a fist fight.

The article concluded with: "On that day, Danny Mason fought for law and order, an end to gang violence in our city. He put himself on the line. On that day, Mayor Danny was our hero."

A fitting epitaph.

She picked up her phone and called Cody's number. When he answered, her heartbeat quickened. Her words tumbled out. "There's something I have to say, even though you don't really believe in politeness. I have to say it. Thank you."

"Tell me in person. Open your door."

In her fuzzy slippers, she ran to the door and flung it wide.

Cody stood there, cell phone in hand. With the collar of his leather jacket turned up and snug Levi's on his long legs, he looked more gorgeous than ever.

She leaped into his arms and hung on tight. She never wanted to be away from him again. Never.

He carried her inside and kicked the door closed. "I've missed you, Rue."

"Me, too."

She released her grip and slipped her feet onto the floor. Looking up at him, she drank in every detail of his features. The grin that lifted the corner of his mouth. The glow from his blue eyes.

"It's Christmas morning," she said. "Why aren't you with your family?"

"I am." His smile broadened. "You're the only one I want to be with."

A warmth filled her from within. "That's the best present I could ever have."

"I can go one better."

He dropped to one knee. In his hand he held a small velvet box. When he opened it, the shimmer of perfect diamond and two other stones blinded her.

"Marry me, Rue."

Without the slightest hesitation, she took the ring. "Yes."

Finally, she had found her family.

* * * * *

Brad shoved the truck into gear and drove to the bottom of the hill, where the road forked. Turn left, and he'd be home in five minutes. Turn right, and he was headed for Indian Rock.

He had no damn business going to Indian Rock.

He had nothing to say to Meg McKettrick, and if he never set eyes on the woman again, it would be two weeks too soon.

He turned right.

He couldn't have said why.

He just drove straight to the Dixie Dog Drive-In.

Back in the day, he and Meg used to meet at the Dixie Dog, by tacit agreement, when either of them had been away. It had been some kind of universe thing, purely intuitive.

Passing familiar landmarks, Brad told himself he ought to turn around. The old days were gone. Things had ended badly between him and Meg anyhow, and she wasn't going to be at the Dixie Dog.

He kept driving.

He rounded a bend, and there was the Dixie Dog. Its big neon sign, a giant hot dog, was all lit up and going through its corny sequence—first it was covered in red squiggles of light, meant to suggest ketchup, and then yellow, for mustard.

Brad pulled into one of the slots next to a speaker, rolled down the truck window and ordered.

A girl roller-skated out with the order about five minutes later.

When she wheeled up to the driver's window, smiling, her eyes went wide with recognition, and she dropped the tray with a clatter.

Silently Brad swore. Damn if he hadn't forgotten he was a famous country singer.

The girl, a skinny thing wearing too much eye makeup, immediately started to cry. "I'm sorry!" she sobbed, squatting to gather up the mess.

"It's okay," Brad answered quietly, leaning to look down at her, catching a glimpse of her plastic name tag. "It's okay, Mandy. No harm done."

"I'll get you another dog and a shake right away, Mr. O'Ballivan!"

"Mandy?"

She stared up at him pitifully, sniffling. Thanks to the copious tears, most of the goop on her eyes had slid south. "Yes?"

"When you go back inside, could you not mention seeing me?"

"But you're Brad O'Ballivan!"

"Yeah," he answered, suppressing a sigh. "I know."

She rolled a little closer. "You wouldn't happen to have a picture you could autograph for me, would you?"

"Not with me," Brad answered.

"You could sign this napkin, though," Mandy said. "It's only got a little chocolate on the corner."

Brad took the paper napkin and her order pen, and scrawled his name. Handed both items back through the window.

She turned and whizzed back toward the side entrance to the Dixie Dog.

Brad waited, marveling that he hadn't considered incidents like this one before he'd decided to come back home. In retrospect, it seemed shortsighted, to say the least, but the truth was, he'd expected to be—Brad O'Ballivan.

Presently Mandy skated back out again, and this time she managed to hold on to the tray.

"I didn't tell a soul!" she whispered. "But Heather and Darlene *both* asked me why my mascara was all smeared." Efficiently she hooked the tray onto the bottom edge of the window.

Brad extended payment, but Mandy shook her head.

"The boss said it's on the house, since I dumped your first order on the ground."

He smiled. "Okay, then. Thanks."

Mandy retreated, and Brad was just reaching for the food when a bright red Blazer whipped into the space beside his. The driver's door sprang open, crashing into the metal speaker, and somebody got out in a hurry.

Something quickened inside Brad.

And in the next moment Meg McKettrick was standing practically on his running board, her blue eyes blazing.

Brad grinned. "I guess you're not over me after all," he said.

Silhouette

SPECIAL EDITION™

brings you a heartwarming
new McKettrick's story from

NEW YORK TIMES BESTSELLING AUTHOR

LINDA LAEL MILLER

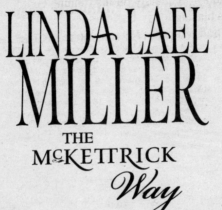

THE MᶜKETTRICK *Way*

Meg McKettrick is surprised to be reunited
with her high school flame, Brad O'Ballivan,
who has returned home to his family's
neighboring ranch. After seeing Meg again,
Brad realizes he still loves her. But the pride
of both manage to interfere with love...until
an unexpected matchmaker gets involved.

—— McKettrick Women ——

Available December wherever you buy books.

Visit Silhouette Books at www.eHarlequin.com SSEIBC24867

REQUEST YOUR FREE BOOKS!

2 FREE NOVELS PLUS 2 FREE GIFTS!

◆ HARLEQUIN®

INTRIGUE®

Breathtaking Romantic Suspense

YES! Please send me 2 FREE Harlequin Intrigue® novels and my 2 FREE gifts. After receiving them, if I don't wish to receive any more books, I can return the shipping statement marked "cancel." If I don't cancel, I will receive 6 brand-new novels every month and be billed just $4.24 per book in the U.S., or $4.99 per book in Canada, plus 25¢ shipping and handling per book and applicable taxes, if any*. That's a savings of close to 15% off the cover price! I understand that accepting the 2 free books and gifts places me under no obligation to buy anything. I can always return a shipment and cancel at any time. Even if I never buy another book from Harlequin, the two free books and gifts are mine to keep forever.

182 HDN EEZ7   382 HDN EEZK

Name	(PLEASE PRINT)	
Address		Apt. #
City	State/Prov.	Zip/Postal Code

Signature (if under 18, a parent or guardian must sign)

Mail to the **Harlequin Reader Service®:**
IN U.S.A.: P.O. Box 1867, Buffalo, NY 14240-1867
IN CANADA: P.O. Box 609, Fort Erie, Ontario L2A 5X3

Not valid to current Harlequin Intrigue subscribers.

Want to try two free books from another line?
Call 1-800-873-8635 or visit www.morefreebooks.com.

* Terms and prices subject to change without notice. NY residents add applicable sales tax. Canadian residents will be charged applicable provincial taxes and GST. This offer is limited to one order per household. All orders subject to approval. Credit or debit balances in a customer's account(s) may be offset by any other outstanding balance owed by or to the customer. Please allow 4 to 6 weeks for delivery.

Your Privacy: Harlequin is committed to protecting your privacy. Our Privacy Policy is available online at www.eHarlequin.com or upon request from the Reader Service. From time to time we make our lists of customers available to reputable firms who may have a product or service of interest to you. If you would prefer we not share your name and address, please check here. ☐

HI07

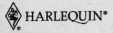

HARLEQUIN®

American ★ *Romance*®

Kate Merrill had grown up convinced
that the most attractive men were incapable
of ever settling down. Yet the harder she
resisted the superstar photographer
Tyler Nichols, the more persistent the
handsome world traveler became.
So by the time Christmas arrived, there
was only one wish on her holiday list—
that she was wrong!

LOOK FOR

THE CHRISTMAS DATE

BY

Michele Dunaway

**Available December
wherever you buy books**

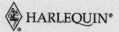

HARLEQUIN®

INTRIGUE®

COMING NEXT MONTH

#1029 UP IN FLAMES by Rita Herron
Nighthawk Island
Detective Bradford Walsh believed only in hard facts. But after saving Rosanna Redhill from a firebug setting Savannah ablaze, was he being led somewhere even more combustible?

#1030 CLASSIFIED CHRISTMAS by B.J. Daniels
Whitehorse, Montana
Cade Jackson had loved Texas girls before, and it led to nothing but trouble. But after new girl in town Andi Blake is kidnapped, it was up to the Montana cowboy to recover a missing three million dollars before the Christmas deadline.

#1031 WOLF MOON by Patricia Rosemoor
The McKenna Legacy
After Rhys Lindgren tried to chase Alieen McKenna back to the big city, she suspected he wasn't all human...but that didn't stop her from reentering the wilderness to break all the boundaries.

#1032 TELLING SECRETS by Tracy Montoya
Search-and-rescue tracker Alex Gray didn't believe Sophie Brennan's predictions—until they began coming true. But would he heed her warnings when his path took them past the Renegade Ridge Mountains to find his missing father?

#1033 ALASKAN FANTASY by Elle James
Would Sam Russell and Kat Sikes outrace a killer on the frozen Alaskan trail, only to find cold comfort in each other?

#1034 THE STRANGER AND I by Carol Ericson
Covert operative Justin Vidal was a man on the edge until Lila Monroe pulled him back. But now her fate rested in the hands of a reckless stranger caught in a web of lethal spies.

www.eHarlequin.com

HICNM1107